FISHING FOR ALMOST ANYTHING THAT MOVES

Mature Content: Rated R

Mark Lee Masters

First Edition 2004

ISBN :   Softcover   1-4134-5280-9

To order additional copies of this book, contact:
Xlibris Corporation
1-888-795-4274
www.Xlibris.com
Orders@Xlibris.com
24684

CONTENTS

ACKNOWLEDGMENTS

My highest praise goes to my teachers who inspired me to write. I must thank my proofreader for being so patient with my impatience. I would also like to thank the people who read the early forms of the book and offered helpful advice. To my wife, I must say that she is truly a tolerant person to put up with me. She is the only reason that I have any time to write. I thank my readers for being there. Yes, some people still enjoy a good book.

CHAPTER ONE

Fishing for Muskies

Jeff Mullet was a big man. I don't mean fat. I mean he had a large frame and his bones and muscles were big. His had piercing brown eyes and a brown mustache that matched what little hair he had left on his head. He usually wore faded blue jeans and a flannel shirt. His favorite shirt was gray and black plaid. It was extra thick material, and he liked how warm it was. On the Sunday afternoon that we find him fishing for muskies, he has on his favorite flannel shirt. Jeff is standing six foot tall, in his 14 foot aluminum boat. He is on Little Lake Tippicanoe, near North Webster, Indiana. Standing makes it easier for him to endure the long hours he puts in fishing in a boat with seats that are low and force the legs to get bunched up and cramped if you sit too long. Jeff would stand for about half an hour and then sit for the same amount of time. On this 13th day of April, 2003, Jeff was fishing on the same spot where the state record musky had been caught on April 1 of 2002. He wasn't concerned about the state record though. He just wanted to catch a muskie that was big and exciting. That was it. He was out for excitement. His friend Bill Ellis was with him. Bill didn't fish. He just went along for the ride. He would help net fish and work the anchor from where he sat in the front of the boat. Jeff often thought how fortunate it was that Bill was along. He made the boat more balanced so that it would plane out better. Besides he made good conversation and liked to make Jeff laugh.

Bill was also a big man. He had a black mustache and steel blue eyes. His eyebrows were quite bushy. He was clean shaven except for the mustache, but he always had five o'clock shadow. He was sitting and talking as Jeff trolled slowly from the back seat. Both men were 48 years old. The boat was aimed to the north and was steering itself at the moment. Bill said, "I've been fishing with you for 10 years now, Jeff, and I still don't see why you like it so much. You usually let the fish go, and you've been fishing for muskies for two years and have only caught a couple small ones. Why do you keep on trying for a big one?" Jeff replied, "I just like being out here with nature. It helps me forget how nasty my factory job is. Plus it helps me get away from my wife's never ending 'honey do' list." Bill shouted, "So there is a method to the madness! I come along with you just to get out on the lake. It is real peaceful on Tippicanoe. It isn't as developed as Wawasee, and there aren't so many large boats to make disturbing wakes that threaten to swamp a small boat like this one."

They finally reached the bank and turned to troll back the opposite direction. Jeff slowed the speed of the trolling motor a little and started to release line, until his 12 inch rubber rainbow trout imitation was about 20 yards behind the boat. Bill said, "That sure is a large lure you're using. Nothing small will even try to take that monster." Jeff said, "That's the idea, I want a giant musky, not a small one." Suddenly Jeff's rod tip dipped down into the water and the reel started screaming as line rushed out into the water. Jeff jerked back hard on the rod twice and then a third time for good measure. Bill asked, "Are you trying to jerk the hook out?" Jeff responded, "I just want to make sure the hook is set good. Sometimes musky just carry the lure a ways and then spit it out. This one is on good!" Jeff pulled up hard on the rod, and then dropped down suddenly, cranking at the reel the whole time. He kept repeating that sequence of actions over and over, but the reel kept giving off a whining noise as line was being ripped from it. Jeff said, "I'm not too worried about running out of line on this Penn 49 trolling reel. I've got 200 yards on 120 lb test braided line spiced to 300 yards of 40 lb test mono. I just have to keep this fish from wrapping itself around some object like a log or rock. I'm going to tighten the drag." He quit cranking for a second and adjusted the drag tighter. The reel started making a lower pitched whine and the boat started moving to the west with the trolling motor shut off.

Bill said, "I thought you shut off the trolling motor. We're moving toward the fish!" Jeff exclaimed, "He's pulling the whole boat along with him!" Jeff kept pulling up on the rod and cranking as he lowered the rod. His muscles were starting to ache. "I wish you had a fishing license Bill, you could help reel this leviathan in. He must be as big as a house! Jeff looked at his reel and could tell that he only had about 50 yards of line left on the spool. He reached over and tightened the drag a little more. He had been fighting the fish for about an hour. As he started reeling faster, the fish changed directions and started heading back to the southeast. Bill asked, "If he manages to get back into the large weed bed in the corner of the lake, we'll have trouble with the line getting tangled won't we?" Jeff replied, "Yes, You're right. I'm cranking like mad to try to get him to the boat before he reaches the weeds. Jeff perspired heavily as he cranked wildly at his reel. Bill looked at his watch. Another 40 minutes had passed and Jeff was starting to look pretty tired. He paused every once in and awhile to rest.

Suddenly the line went slack and Jeff stated, "I think I've lost him." He started reeling line in like mad. "I'm going to try to get back as much line as I can. He may just be swimming towards the boat now." In a couple minutes the line tightened and the rod jerked. "I've still got him on. He's heading back for the weeds again!" The boat slid through the water after the fish. It weighed over a hundred pounds with the motor, but it was being dragged along at considerable speed by a fish. Jeff shouted, "This must be the biggest musky that has ever been caught!" Bill retorted, "It sure isn't any bluegill or bass!" They both sat in the boat now. Jeff didn't want to fall overboard in his excitement. He said, "If I had one of those big bass boats, we wouldn't be dragged around like this. But we wouldn't be able to work in such shallow water either." Now he got quiet and started looking real determined. He cranked and cranked at his reel.

Finally the fish jumped out of the water about 100 feet from the boat. Jeff stated, "Make sure the net is free, Bill. I don't want him to break the line when we get him close to the boat." Bill picked up the net and held it at the ready. He was getting excited. He said, "How heavy do you think this one is, Jeff?" Jeff said, "It could top 60 or 70 pounds. I'm glad I brought my biggest net. It will come in handy today. Jeff tightened the drag one last time and began to reel the musky in close to the boat. When the musky saw the boat close up, and could see Jeff and Bill, it made one last effort. It splashed mightily and quickly took out several hundred yards of line. Bill said, "I didn't think he was quite finished yet. Bill, could I ask you to get me a coke out of the cooler? I'm getting pretty thirsty. You'll have to hold it up to my lips. I can't let go of this rod and reel." Bill grabbed a coke and held the bottle up to Jeff's mouth. He gulped greedily and coke poured down the front of his shirt. He didn't seem to notice. He just kept on cranking on the reel. Bill said, "You're lucky that we're doing this in April and not August. You would be suffering quite a bit, working this hard in such heat. It's only about 70 degrees today." Jeff replied, "Yes, that's something to be grateful for. I'm grateful for this big fish too. But, I'll be even more pleased, if I ever get it in the boat.

Bill drank a coke silently and watched Jeff working on the musky. Finally he dipped the empty bottle into the lake and filled it with water. He poured the water on Jeff's reel. It was so hot from friction that it steamed a little when the water hit it. Jeff said, "Thanks, Bill. That should help keep the discs in the drag from burning up." Bill replied, "My father used to catch some big trout out on Lake Michigan. That's how I knew about cooling off the reel." They both got quiet for awhile and watched the line as it slowly came out of the water and back onto the reel. Finally Bill started talking a little more about his father. He said, "My father liked to take charter boats out of Grand Haven. One captain of a boat called the Thunder Buck, really knew how to help people catch lots of big fish. I believe his name was Captain Will. His boat was 31 feet long and she could handle the large waves of Lake Michigan without making you seasick. I went with my dad on several of those charters. We caught mostly lake trout that were a little over 20 pounds. But I remember one that my dad hooked that must have weighed over 40 pounds. It took out almost all the line from the reel. The reel had a line counter that said the trout took out 600 yards of line.

My dad asked Captain Will to turn the boat and move toward the fish. The Captain did so reluctantly. He said that it would not be a record if you had to motor toward the fish. It was against the rules for area records. Dad said that he only wanted to keep from loosing the line to the fish. That much line is expensive. When he got about half of the line back, the captain stopped the boat. He didn't like stopping the boat or turning sharply, because that meant he had to reel in all six lures that were out. It was extra trouble for him. He was willing to do it this time, since dad agreed that he wouldn't try to claim a record with his catch. Dad pulled and pulled on the rod, much like you are doing today. After a ten minute standoff, where the fish wouldn't give an inch, the hook came loose and dad lost the fish. It still made a good story to tell about the one that got away." Just then the musky jumped again. He was only about 50 feet from the boat. Bill readied the net. As the big fish drew in close, both men got excited and stood up in the boat. When they leaned over to net the fish, the boat tipped precariously. They both fell to the bottom of the boat. They scrambled to their feet, delighted that they had not gone overboard into the cold April water. The musky was still waiting there beside the boat. It was exhausted. Bill swooped over its head with the net. A third of the fish wouldn't fit into the net. Jeff helped drag it aboard.

Bill grabbed for the camera and Jeff held up the heavy fish by the gills. After they each got their picture taken with the fish, they measured it and weighed it. It weighed 46 pounds and was 48 inches long. They had never heard of a Muskellunge that long or that heavy in Indiana. Jeff carefully lowered the fish over the side. He knew it would have put him in the record book, but he wanted someone else to get a chance with that fish. He didn't need fame. He had his picture of himself with the fish. The musky moved its tail slowly as it swam off towards the weed bed.

Jeff and Bill motored over the main Lake Tippicanoe and used the fish finder to locate a school of bluegill. The bluegill were in shallow water about eight feet deep on the south end of the lake where the bottom was nice and sandy. Jeff started to pull in one after the other. They were all about 9 to 10 inches long. They were good keepers. He did catch a few smaller bluegill. Jeff always wet his hands before he took hold of the fish. He wanted to preserve the slime on the fish. He knew that a dry hand on a fish causes the fish to become diseased. After catching about 40 bluegill, Jeff asked Bill to pass him a sandwich from the cooler. They both ate a sandwich. Both men started to clean some of the fish right there in the boat. They had brought a camp stove, cast iron skillet and butter with them. Jeff liked to eat some of his catch as soon as he caught them. They threw the entrails into a plastic bag and pushed them under a seat. It wasn't long until the fish were sizzling in butter. Bill reached in his jacket pocket and pulled out a salt shaker. "I thought you might want this, he said. You always like to salt your food heavily. It's a good idea now. It'll help keep you from getting cramps." Jeff replied, "Thanks. That was good thinking." He reached for the shaker and salted the fish liberally. Bill continued, "I also brought bread. Bluegill taste the best when you sandwich them between slices of buttered bread." Jeff replied, "You're right about that. You thought of everything today." Bill said, "Well I try. I'm grateful that you don't make me fish. So I try to make other contributions."

Jeff said, "I still don't see why you don't like to fish. It's all I can think about." Bill replied, "I like reading and writing. I can read a Hemmingway story about fishing, and get as much enjoyment as I would if I were really fishing, and I don't have to buy lots of equipment." Jeff rebutted, "I only paid $60.00 for the musky rod. That's not a lot of money." Bill said, "But I don't work at a job. I just cut wood to heat the house. My wife works part time. That's quite a bit of money to us. You spend money like it's going out of style. I don't even buy books very often. I take them from the library, or I buy them cheaply on the internet." Jeff said, "You have a $1,000 computer don't you?" Bill said, "I bought that when I was still working. I just can't stand sweat shops anymore. They drive people so hard it's ridiculous. They constantly threaten to punish workers if they don't produce enough. I'd rather live frugally and skip the work scene." Jeff said, "I hate my factory job as much as you've hated jobs. I plan on retiring when I'm 62. That way I should have a few years to fish full time before I die. What's the point of dying on the job of a heart attack? It happens to more people than you would think. They scrimp and save for their retirement and then never make it to retirement. That's tragic isn't it?" Jeff replied, "You're right about that."

Suddenly the camp stove lit some fumes from the boat's leaking gas line. The stern of the boat burst into a fireball. It quickly spread to the front of the boat. Both men instinctively jumped overboard. They were in about 5 feet of water, so they could stand up and watch the fire from the water. The top of the plastic gas tank melted through in a couple of minutes. This caused the boat to explode in a dramatic burst of flames. The water was terribly cold. They quickly swam to the closest back where there were houses. There was a light on in the first house and they ran up to the house and knocked on the door. An attractive young blond woman answered the door and looked alarmed when she saw them. She said, "I saw the fire on your boat. It's a wonder that you are both alive. I called 911. They should be here in a few minutes." Jeff said, "I don't think we really need an ambulance. I think that we just got some hair burned off our heads and hands."

The woman said, "My name is Lilly Schrock. You must both take off your shirts so that I can see if you are badly burned. I'll turn up the thermostat so you can warm up. I don't want either of you going into shock." They obligingly took off their shirts. She looked them over closely and said, "You're both very lucky, or maybe God was watching out for you. You both have some blisters on your hands and faces. You will probably be perfectly fine in a couple of weeks." Jeff said, "I sure hate it that I lost the camera with the picture of the musky in it. No one will believe that it was so big." Lilly said, "Don't worry about your silly camera. You're lucky to be alive. What started the fire?" Bill said, "We were trying to cook some fish on the boat. It never occurred to us that the boat's fuel supply might catch on fire. I guess there was a leak in the fuel line." Lilly said, "It was very foolish to have fire on a boat. But I won't lecture you anymore. You've paid for your mistake, dearly." Jeff said, "I was wanting to buy a better boat. At least now I have an excuse to buy one." Lilly said, "Now I've heard everything. Maybe you are a little delirious from the accident. I'll get each of you a blanket to wrap up in. Then I'll make some hot coffee. It will help to warm you up."

Lilly went into the next room and returned in a minute carrying two blankets. She wrapped one around each of the men. Then she started making the coffee. She put two cups of water in the microwave and had hot water ready in just a minute. She spooned some instant Folgers into each cup and then asked, "Do either of you take milk or sugar in your coffee. They both said in two part harmony, "Black, please." As they sipped their coffee, she asked them for their names. They introduced themselves, and then stepped over to the window to watch their boat burn out on the lake. The anchor rope had burned off, and the boat was now moving with the wind, out into the middle of the lake. They could hear the sirens of the ambulance and the fire trucks. This was turning into quite an interesting day of fishing indeed! They were whisked away by the ambulance. The fire department decided to let the fire burn out. They kept an eye on the boat to make sure that it didn't get pushed by the wind into another boat or other flammable object.

They were treated at Goshen General Hospital and released the same day. Jeff called his wife to come and get them. He said to Bill, "I guess we'll know not to cook food on the boat next time, right?" Bill said, "I don't even want to think about it!" Jeff replied,

"At least you can go with me tomorrow and look at new boats."
Bill said, "Well, I guess so; if my wife isn't too strongly opposed
to it. She's going to get hysterical when she hears about this. Jeff
said, "It could have happened to anyone. We didn't know the
stupid gas line was leaking." Bill retorted, "Well, just remember
to tell my wife that it wasn't my idea to cook fish on the boat."

Jeff's wife arrived and scolded him for being so reckless.
Then she started to cry. She said, "You could have both be burned
to death. What saved you?" Bill said, "We both jumped into the
water before the fire had a chance to kill us." She said, "Well
thank God for quick thinking!" I'm glad you're both alive. What
about the boat?" Jeff said, "I'm glad you mentioned the boat,
honey. I'd like to go out and buy a new 14 foot boat tomorrow;
with a 40 horse power engine. The old boat is a total loss.
Everything burned." Jeff's wife, Nancy, said, "I can't believe that
you're already planning to buy another boat! Just promise me
that you won't cook on it. No one will even smoke a cigar on the
boat. Is that understood?" Jeff said, "Yes dear, I promise."

The next morning Jeff and Bill were up early shopping for a
new boat. They lived close to a boat factory and were able to get
a nice discount on a boat, motor and trailer. Since Jeff had called
off sick because of his blisters, they decided to take the new boat
out fishing. They went to Syracuse Lake, which is only about 10
miles north of Lake Tippicanoe. They were on the water early. It
was still dark and there were no other boats at the boat launch.
Jeff said, "Most people have to work today. I think I'll milk this
blister thing for as long as my doctor will let me. In fact, our near
demise has made me think about how short life can be. I think
I'll just retire, so that you and I can fish whenever we want to.
After all, I have plenty of money. Why work any longer?" Bill
said, "Now you're starting to see things my way."

They launched the boat, and headed for the east end of the
lake. The new Mercury boat motor gave off a wonderful familiar
sound as it sped them across the lake at the maximum 7 m.p.h.
for night time driving. They arrived at Jeff's favorite spot in just a
few minutes. Bill lowered the electric anchor and Jeff baited his

hook with a wax worm. Bill read a book about fishing by Ernest Hemingway. Jeff said, "I sure wish you'd try fishing a little." Bill said, "I am fishing, in my mind. I'm reeling in a giant blue marlin off the east coast of Cuba. Someone keeps bringing me drinks and coaching me on how to play the fish. I'm having a wonderful time." Jeff replied, "Hey. That sounds pretty good. I'd like to read that one when you're done with it." Bill said, "I'll have it finished today. Then you can have it." Jeff's bobber went under, and he pulled up suddenly on his rod. He had a 9 foot St. Croix rod. It bent noticeably under the weight of a 10 inch bluegill. He carefully removed his hook and placed the fish in a cooler full of ice water. Bill said, "Why do you always keep the fish in ice water? What's wrong with a stringer or bucket full of lake water?" Jeff said, "I like to know for sure that my fish are still fresh when the long day of fishing is over. I don't want to take any chances on food poisoning. Since I have the cooler open, do you want something to drink? I've got cold pop and some Miller Lite." Bill said, "I'll take a coke. It's too early for beer. I'll wait till the sun gets hot for that." Jeff passed a coke over to Bill. He opened it and guzzled down about half of it.

At about 8:00 o'clock Jeff started to catch one big bluegill after another. There were some crappie and bass too. Most of the bass were too small. He carefully released them so they would grow bigger. He was always sure to wet his hands before he took hold of a bass. He didn't want to ruin the slime layer on the fish. He wouldn't know whether he was going to keep it or not, until he measured it.

After he had about a dozen fish, he said to Bill, "I only want to catch what I need for one meal. I don't believe in making a hog of myself. Some people catch forty a day and then the fish go stale in the freezer. That's wasteful. I believe in leaving some fish for other people to catch. Are you and your wife going to come over tonight for a fish fry? If you do, I could justify catching another dozen fish." Bill said, "I'm sure my wife would love that. Go ahead and catch some more." Jeff kept on fishing, and by 10:00 o'clock he had 24 good sized fish. Jeff said, "Let's cruise around for a couple hours and watch the fish finder. I want to see where fish are located in the rest of the lake. We can go through the channel and scout out Lake Wawasee too." Bill replied, "Let's stop at the frog tavern for some burgers and fries." Jeff said, "That sounds like a good plan. We can drink a couple cold ones and then cruise the lakes some more looking for fish. Around 4:00 o'clock we can go to my place and clean the fish." Bill said, "Let me use your cell phone to call my wife. I need to make sure she can go to your house for supper tonight." Jeff handed over the cell phone. In a few seconds Bill was talking to his wife. "Sandy, can we eat fish at Bill's house tonight? He caught a large mess of fish this morning and we'd like to eat them while they are fresh." Bill told Jeff, "She said she'd love to come over tonight. She says she'll call Nancy to plan the rest of the meal." Jeff said, "Great, my wife will like this. She loves fried fish." Bill closed the phone and handed it back to Jeff.

Jeff said, "Tonight I'll tell Nancy about my plan for early retirement. She knows that I don't like work. I just have to explain to her how our savings can easily tide us over till I become old enough for social security. She'll love the idea of me having more energy to do her "honey do" lists. And she'll like the nonstop flow of fresh fish for the table. She knows I've been wanting to spend more time fishing." Bill asked, "How exactly do you plan on convincing your wife to let you retire at age forty-eight?" Jeff said, "I'll use the calculator. When she sees that we can use $10,000 per year of our $140,000 savings to pay expenses till I'm sixty-two, it will be clear to her. Why struggle to keep all our savings when we have social security to fall back on? Why not enjoy life?" She likes her job. She can keep working as long as she wants to."

Bill said, "Well, you have your house paid for. You should be able to live with one income and $10,000 from savings. You just reach a certain point in your life when you need less work and more fishing. If you want to earn some money you could pick up something part time." Jeff laughed and said, "I doubt if that will be too tempting right away. But, you never know how retirement is going to affect you. Everyone is different. I just can't imagine getting tired of fishing and wanting to go back to work." Bill said, "Yes, that's hard to imagine. Neither of us has a record of loving work."

That evening at Jeff's house, Bill and his wife Sandy ate fish with their friends once again. It was a frequent occurrence. Jeff mentioned his plan of retiring early, right off the bat. Nancy was not happy about the idea at first, but she warmed to the idea when he explained how their savings would last until social security started. He also mentioned about how he would have plenty of time to help with work around the house. Finally she agreed. Since he couldn't find any work that was pleasant, why not retire early. They played cards till midnight and then went their separate ways. Jeff and Bill agreed to go fishing again the next morning at 5:00 o'clock. Jeff wanted to try for another picture of a large musky.

The night passed quickly, and soon Jeff and Bill were heading for North Webster in Jeff's SL2 Saturn. It was a small car, but it had no trouble pulling the light aluminum boat. They went a mile past North Webster and turned right. They took a country road for about 5 miles until they arrived at Grassy Creek boat launch. It was a public boat launch that wasn't very crowded because of its remote location. Also, the creek was shallow and narrow at places. Most of the big bass boats were a little worried about hitting bottom. The creek led north to Lake Tippicanoe and south to a series of other smaller lakes. Jeff and Bill headed north to Tippicanoe. The creek snaked its way through cattails and lillypads for a 20 minute ride until it emptied into the south end of Lake Tippicanoe. Jeff headed the boat east to a channel that led to small Lake Tippicanoe. The channel entered the lake on the northwest corner. They steered the boat quickly to the southeast end of the lake. They went right to the spot where they had hooked the giant musky. Jeff put in the trolling motor and they started trolling along the large weed bed at that corner of the lake.

Jeff said, "I would like to go fishing on Lake Superior this spring. Do you want to come along, Bill?" Bill replied, "Sure, why not. It sounds interesting. Are you planning on going to the Canadian side or the Michigan side?" Jeff said, "I would like to go to the Canadian side. There's a spot called Chipawana bay. My Uncle Les and Aunt Erma Gamp have a fishing lodge there. I've heard that the perch fishing is great, and Aunt Erma is a great cook. They'd give us a discount since I'm related to them. We can stay for three days for about $200.00 with everything included. I'll pay for everything. We can take the Saturn. It gets great gas mileage." Bill said, "You're very generous. I think I'll even try a little fishing if your uncle is providing the equipment." Jeff said, "Well, he expects us to bring our own rods, but I'll buy you a rod and reel. A combo set is only about $40.00." Bill said, "Thanks. I promise to use it. I won't read at all while we're on the boat." Jeff said, "That's very considerate of you. I appreciate it." Bill said, "When do you want to go?" Jeff said, "I'd like to leave tomorrow if we can. We can buy you the rod and reel this evening and I'll call Les and tell him we're coming. They won't be booked up this week. It's still quite cold that far north. Most people book for May or later."

Just then, Jeff's rod dipped suddenly. He had another musky, or maybe it was the same one. He jerked hard on the rod to set the hook. The musky felt the pain of the hook set and jumped from the water. Jeff fought the fish for over 30 minutes. Bill helped him land it with the net. It was a 40 ponder that measured over 36 inches. Bill took several pictures of Jeff with the musky. Jeff didn't need to be told to smile. He was obviously happy about his catch. He said, "Even if it isn't as big as the other musky, it was fun to catch, and at least I'll get a picture this time." Bill said, "You'd better let it go before it gets too short on oxygen." Jeff said, "You're right." He leaned over the edge of the boat with the heavy fish and released it. It swam away eagerly and showed no weakness from its ordeal.

Jeff said, "Let's head for home now. I want to buy that rod and reel. I love buying fishing equipment. Also, I can't wait to call my uncle and tell him we're coming." Bill said, "Don't forget to pull up the trolling motor." Jeff responded, "Oh, Yeah. Thanks for the reminder. I don't want it flying off and heading for the bottom of the lake." Jeff pushed the boat to maximum speed as they headed for the channel that would take them to the main Lake Tippecanoe. They slowed for the channel and the sped across the south end of Tippecanoe. When they got to the mouth of Grassy Creek, they saw a shapely woman in her yard sun bathing in a bikini. It was Lilly Schrock, the woman who had called the ambulance for them and warmed them in her house. They waved and pulled up to her boat dock. She ran over to them and said, "I see you two are already out fishing again. I hope you won't be doing any cooking!" Jeff said, "We will never cook on a boat again." She said, "That's wonderful, will you take me for a ride." "Jump in." said Jeff. She climbed in and sat in the middle seat. Jeff opened the throttle wide and the boat surged out into the lake. The waves were a little rough. Lilly's scantily clad body bounced in an alluring manner as they rode around the lake. Finally Jeff brought the boat back to her pier. He said, "I'm sorry that we can't stay longer, but we have to prepare for a fishing trip to Ontario, Canada. We're leaving tomorrow." Lilly said, "Just like men, always in a hurry to leave. Promise me you will both drop by again. If I'm not in the yard come knock on the door. I'll make you both a cup of coffee." She gave each of them a hug and a kiss. A long wet kiss. Then she walked back to her lawn chair and started sunning herself some more.

Jeff started the motor and headed up Grassy Creek. Bill said, "How do I tell my wife about this?" Jeff said, "It might be best to just forget to mention it. I know I'm not telling my wife unless you tell yours." They rode the boat slowly up the creek as Bill told Jeff jokes. When they got back to New Paris they parked the boat in Jeff's drive way. Jeff called his uncle and made arrangements. Then he took Bill to Wal-Mart and bought him a rod and reel. Both were made in China, but they seemed to be of good quality. Jeff said, "Almost anything you buy nowadays is made in China, but they are made to American specifications. I think you won't have any trouble reeling in perch with this outfit. Sometimes the reel gives out from bringing the perch up from over 140 feet down." Then he thought a minute. "I guess we'd better get you an American made reel. The rod will be good enough, I think." He picked out a Shakespeare reel and handed it to Bill. "This one is only $20.00 and it should be good enough." Bill held the rod and reel. "Thanks, he said. I'm already getting excited about this trip."

They took the equipment to Bill's house at 11th and Division St. in New Paris. Bill lived on the northwest corner of the intersection and Jeff lived across the street on the northeast corner. Jeff lived in a brown two story brick house. Bill's house was a smaller two story wood house with light yellow siding. Bill went in the house to tell his wife about the Canada fishing trip. She said, "I thought you didn't like to fish." Bill said, "Jeff bought me a rod and reel. So I'm going to try it. He says that we'll bring home lots of perch. Some people catch hundreds of them." Sandy said, "When are you going to return?" Jeff said, "We'll only fish for three days. It's a two day drive each way. So we'll be home in seven days." Sandy said, "I don't mind if you go, Bill, but you have to fix the toilet when you come home. It's been making a funny sound for a week now. I don't want it to make our pump work a lot." Bill said, "I'll fix it the minute I get back."

Jeff went home and told Nancy about his plan to go to Canada fishing. She said, "I just want you to enjoy life. It wasn't good for you to be unhappy like you were when you were working. That kind of unhappiness can make you sick. We have enough money to live on. You just go and have a good time. Don't spend too much money though. I'll pack you some food so that you don't spend too much time in restaurants." Jeff said, "That's a good idea. I like egg salad. I'd also like plenty of fruit like bananas and apples. Oranges would be good too."

Nancy packed food into a cooler while Jeff packed his suit case. Jeff went to the kitchen and told Nancy, "I caught a nice musky today. This time I'll have the picture to prove it. I dropped the film off at Wal-Mart. Would you pick up the pictures on Thursday in the afternoon?" Nancy said, "I'll get them. I want to see the big fish. Will you take out the trash? Tomorrow is Tuesday and the trash will be collected." Jeff said, "Sure, I'll get that right away." He kissed her on the lips and gave her a hug. He said, "I never thought that I would like retirement, but I can see that it will be fun since I'm still young enough to enjoy it." He bagged up the trash and then lit a fire in the fireplace. He said, "It's supposed to get down to 40 degrees tonight. A fire will be nice. I have to get to bed early. Bill and I are leaving at 5:00 o'clock in the morning. We want to make it to the Canadian border by supper time. We'll find a place to stay in Canada. The rates are cheaper there because of the favorable currency exchange."

Jeff fell asleep by the fire. After several hours, the sun set and the fire was looking nice and romantic. Nancy shut off all the lights and curled up next to Jeff on the floor. They were lying on a nice soft white bear skin rug. She kissed Jeff on the lips and started pulling his clothing off. It had been awhile since they had made love in front of the fire. The warmth of the fire caused Jeff to nod off for a little while. Jeff woke up when Nancy started heavy petting with him. He just lay still and let her do what she wanted to do. She was more excited than usual since she knew that she wouldn't see him for a week. She really let herself go. She was still quite limber for a 48 year old. She didn't get tired for several hours. Jeff watched her in the fire light as she did all her favorite things to him. Finally at midnight, they went up stairs, showered and went to bed.

At Bill's house the same sort of thing was going on. Only they had a small wood burning stove instead of a fireplace. Bill and Sandy had packed the suitcase together. When the sun went down they fired up the wood stove and stripped naked. They gave each other back rubs in front of the fire. Once they were relaxed, they kissed for a long time with Bill lying on top. He gave her a hickey to remember him by. Then he took her in many different ways. She loved variety. After several hours of fun, they fell asleep right there in front of the fire.

CHAPTER TWO

The Canadian Experience

Jeff was up at 5:00 o'clock and called Bill who was still in front of the fire place. Bill answered the phone and promised to be ready in ten minutes. He threw on his clothes and took his new fishing rod and reel right over to Jeff's house. They road off to Canada in Jeff's 1999 Saturn SL2. He loved the gas mileage and the stylish all plastic body. That is except the hood, which suffered one little rust spot which he touched up regularly. The hood was metal for some mysterious reason. He hated rust, and would probably buy an all plastic car if it was offered to him at a reasonable price. He longed for a Corvette with its all fiberglass body, but he couldn't justify paying such a high sticker price. As Jeff and Bill headed north into Michigan, Jeff watched the scenery and told fishing stories. Bill set the cruise control at 85 m.p.h. and they blasted up highway 131 towards the big lake. Bill told crazy jokes as he drove. His jokes were always ridiculous and were only funny because they were so stupid. Bill told one joke that he told often, "What's yellow and goes bang bang bang bang? A four door banana." Then he would laugh with a funny cackle. His laughter was funnier than the joke, by far. He always laughed at his own jokes. Finally Jeff would give in and started laughing too. "Laughter is contagious even when it's insane laughter, I guess," said Jeff.

They stopped in the town of Cadillac, at a road side table, and ate some of the food Jeff's wife had sent along. There was a cool spring breeze blowing, and frogs were croaking in the ditch along the road side. Jeff stated, "Well we've traveled over 200 miles in only three hours. We're making good time." Bill said, "Yes, I can't wait to see the Mackinac Bridge. It's over five miles long and 552 feet above the water." Jeff asked, "If you've never been to the bridge, how do you know so much about it?" Bill answered, "A friend gave me a coffee cup with the bridge and relevant facts on it. I drink so much coffee in that cup, that I've memorized most of the facts about the bridge."

They finished their food and drove rapidly towards the bridge. Jeff was testing the Saturn to see when the governor kicked in. He had the car up to 110 m.p.h. at times, when the road was clear of much traffic. Just then he noticed in his mirror that a police car was pulling onto the road behind him. He laid on the brakes and slowed to the speed limit. Luckily for him, the policeman hadn't had his radar turned on. He was sure that it was on now. He obeyed the speed limit for the rest of the way to the bridge. He was afraid the policeman might have radioed ahead for the police to watch for his car. They crossed the bridge slowly so that they could enjoy the view of the water and shoreline.

Since they were ahead of schedule, they drove along the coastline of the north end of Lake Michigan. There were people having campfires on the beach, which was undeveloped. It looked like fun. Jeff said, "I'd like to bring my wife up here for a fire on the beach some evening. There aren't many people here and the scenery is excellent." Bill replied, "I'm sure my wife would like it too. Maybe later this summer we could all come up here together." Jeff responded, "Sounds good." They drove a little further down the road and found a small public campground on the beach. Jeff said, "That looks like it would be a great place to stay the night when we come here with our wives. We could bring tents and rough it." Bill said, "Sounds great. My wife would love that." They investigated the campsite and then headed back towards Chippawanna bay, where Uncle Les and Aunt Erma had their fishing camp.

They arrived at the camp at about 7:00 o'clock in the evening. Uncle Les was at the edge of a wooded area between the road and the cabin. Jeff went over to him and asked what he was doing. He said, "I'm burying the garbage. If we leave it in the garbage can over night, black bears come and dig through it. They can smell it a long ways away, and come to find something to eat." Les was a large man about 65 years old, with gray hair and a shape that said he was well fed. He breathed heavily as he shoveled dirt back over the garbage that he was burying. He stopped for a moment and shook their hands. He said, "I'm Les Gamp. It's good to see you again Jeff. Is this your friend Bill Ellis that you told me about?" Jeff answered, "Yes. This is Bill Ellis. I've known him all my life. Until now, he hasn't fished, but he has watched me fish a lot. He's got his own rod and reel now, and he's eager to catch some perch." Bill said, "I hear there are lots of big perch here on Chippawanna bay." Les said, "Yes, you came at a good time. The barometer has been rising and the fish should be biting. We're also at half moon. That helps with the fishing some, I believe." Bill said, "I've heard about the barometer having an effect on fishing, but I didn't know about the moon. Why does it affect fishing?" Les said, "With most fish, they can see at night better during a full moon. They feed all night, and aren't hungry during the day when we usually fish for them. I've learned from experience that the half moon is a good time to fish. I'm not sure why. It just is. The new moon isn't too bad for fishing, but the half moon is better."

They walked over to the cabin and Aunt Erma met them at the door. She was a white haired kind looking lady who obviously liked her own cooking. She was heavy, but strong looking. She went right to the kitchen and started cooking some beef stew. Then she set the table. She said, "You can both sleep in the attic. We save the other cabin for warmer weather, and for when we don't know the fishermen. You'll be nice and warm in the attic. The beds have goose down comforters that will keep you warm." The men went out to the lake front and watched the sunset while supper was being prepared. Les said, "You're my first clients this year. I just finished getting the boat ready. It'll be great to get back out on the lake. It's been a long winter. Erma and I take the boat to Florida during the winter. We travel to the Atlantic on the St. Laurence seaway and then follow the coastline to St. Petersburg where we own a small bungalow." Bill said, "That sounds like a wonderful lifestyle." Les replied, "We enjoy ourselves. It only cost me three thousand dollars to build this place in 1953. So I don't have borrowed money to worry about. We earn enough during the summer to live on all year round."

Jeff said, "I just retired this week. Nancy and I agreed that we have enough money now that I don't need to work anymore. I just have to keep my spending low so that I can afford to continue not working." Les said, "Early retirement is good if you can keep busy and not get bored. Some people need work to keep them occupied." Jeff said, "I plan on fishing for the rest of my life. I know how to travel cheaply, and fishing is what I've always wanted to do." Bill said, "I quit working fifteen years ago. I couldn't stand the people in the factories. They are so eager to make life rough on other people. My wife works part time, and we know how to live cheaply. I read most of the time, and I do a little writing too." Les said, "What do you write about?" Bill said, "I'm writing detective stories and espionage thrillers so far, but I plan on trying many different types of writing. I don't want to get in a rut and only write one type of story."

Erma's voice echoed across the lake as she called them to supper. "Come on in and eat now," she called. They took one last look at the red sun reflecting off the lake and then went into the log cabin to eat. The smell of beef stew filled the cabin, and there was a warm fire in the black woodstove that stood in the middle of the cabin. They all sat down to eat after they had washed their hands. Les said grace, and then they all ate stew. Erma asked, "What do you do for a living, Bill?" He said, "I'm retired. I write books to keep myself occupied, and I go with Jeff when he fishes. I'm just starting to fish. I used to just go along to watch." Erma said, "Well, you came to the right place to start fishing. Once you feel the tug of those fish on the line, it becomes addicting. There is the thrill of pulling them up and wondering how big they will be and whether they will get away or not. Also, perch are delicious to eat. We can cook up tomorrow's catch as soon as you men get them cleaned." Les said, "Erma likes fishing as much as I do. We like to fish for pike along the shoreline up here. There are some big ones out there! After we catch some perch, we can try for pike. There are rainbow trout up on the mountain lake that isn't far from here." Jeff replied, "That sounds good. I like about any kind of fishing there is." Bill said, "It will be great to catch a variety of fish. My wife will be surprised. I told her we were just going for perch."

Jeff asked, "Do you have television up here?" Erma said, "No. We like it primitive here. We can play some hearts if you want to stay up awhile before going to bed." Jeff said, "I'd like to play hearts. I haven't played that game for years." Bill said, "I like playing hearts. Where do we play?" Les replied, "We play right here on the kitchen table." Erma pulled out a drawer and got the cards. They played for several hours. No one talked much. They were all intent upon winning. Each one of them concentrated on their cards. After about an hour, it was clear that Erma was the best card player. She knew just which cards to keep and which to pass on to the person next to her. Finally they all agreed that it was time for bed. Les said, "I'll wake you up at 5:00 o'clock so we can get an early start. It takes about an hour to get to the first fishing spot." Jeff said, "Good. I like starting out early. I want to see the sunrise from the water." Les pulled down the ladder to the attic, and Bill and Jeff crawled up to the feather beds. They both fell asleep right away. It had been a long drive to Chippawanna bay. They would have a full day ahead of them.

At 5:00 o'clock Les called to the two fishermen, "It's time to come for breakfast. Wake up now." Jeff called down the stairs, "I'm up. I'm awake." He shook Bill and said, "Get up. It's time for breakfast. You're going to become a fisherman." Bill responded, "I hear you. Don't worry. I'm getting up. I'm hungry as a bear." They both got dressed quickly and crawled down the ladder. Erma had a big breakfast waiting for them. They sat down and ate their fill of scrambled eggs and bacon. There was homemade bread and homemade apple butter. They thanked Erma for the breakfast and followed Les to the boat garage. The boat looked old, but well cared for. It was a 24 foot cabin cruiser with twin 60 horsepower Johnson outboards. They crawled into the boat and listened to the engines as they started. It was a familiar and pleasant sound. Les carefully backed the boat out of the garage and turned it around in the channel. They followed the short channel out to the lake. Les throttled up the engines and they headed south along the shoreline, several hundred yards out from shore.

After about half an hour, Les turned the boat out to the west and headed for deeper water. The lake was calm and there were no big waves. They watched the seagulls. Les said, "The seagulls congregate where there are bait fish. The perch are eating the bait fish. All we need to do is watch for the gulls." He steered the boat slowly so as not to disturb the normal behavior of the gulls. After about 20 minutes he stopped the boat and started getting the bait out. He also set out the cooler for keeping the fish in. He used a one ounce sinker to test the depth of the water. Les stated, "I could never justify spending the money on a fish finder. I do things the way I always have done them." He smiled and lowered the sinker at the end of his fishing rod. He said, "Each turn of the reel handle is one foot. There are six feet to a fathom." His weather beaten hands cranked up the sinker from the bottom. "It's 120 feet deep here. Twenty fathoms. The perch often feed just off the bottom, but we can try different depths till we locate them."

Jeff helped Bill set up his tackle. They used two number 6 hooks per line. The hooks were on 12 inch dropper lines. Lines that extended from the main line. The bottom dropper line was fastened 12 inches above a quarter ounce bell sinker which was fastened to the very end of the line. Les showed them how he preferred to place the hook into the minnow. He hooked it through the back so it would continue swimming around in a natural manner. If the minnow wasn't moving, it wouldn't be as likely to get a bite. Les fished with them. It wasn't long till they started catching perch on the small minnows they were using. Bill caught his first fish, and was visibly pleased with it. Jeff measured it for him and said, "It's 12 inches long. A nice perch!" Bill stated, "I'm starting to get the hang of this." Les said, "Keep your lines in the water. We need to get as many fish as we can before the perch move on. They feed in schools. Once they decide to move, we may have trouble finding them again." They all concentrated on keeping their hooks baited and their lines in the water. Jeff pulled in two 12 inch perch at the same time. Next, Bill pulled in two at once. They were reeling in fish as fast as they could. When the perch came up, their air bladders were in their mouths. Les said, "The air bladder comes up in their mouth because of the sudden change in pressure as you bring them up."

In about three hours time they had 101 perch that were all about 12 inches long. Suddenly the fish stopped biting. Les said, "I think a pike has chased away the perch. If you want to you can fish for the pike, Jeff. I brought a pike rod along and a red devil lure." Jeff said, "Sure. I'll give it a try." Les brought out a stout pike rod with a high capacity reel. He proudly opened his tackle box and picked out a ¾ ounce red devil lure. He handed it to Jeff and said, "Good luck. I've caught quite a few pike on this lure."

Jeff tied on the lure with a Trilene knot followed by three half hitches. He wanted to be sure not to lose his uncle's favorite lure. Losing a good pike wouldn't be good either. He started making long casts in every direction trying to cover as much water a possible. On one cast the boat drifted over the line so that the lure was pulled under the boat. Bill was watching as the lure passed under the boat. A large pike was right behind the lure, following it under the boat. Just as Jeff was pulling the lure to the surface, the pike struck it and ran with it. The line surged off the reel. Bill was still thinking about how there had been two pike. The first one was about four feet long. The one following it had been even longer. To him it had appeared to be six feet long. He didn't have any idea how long pike could get. He was pretty sure he had seen the biggest pike that ever existed. It was the one that got away. He told Jeff all about the second giant pike, as Jeff reeled with determination and tried to bring in the small four foot pike that he had on the line.

Jeff's fun with the pike went on for a long time. He said, "This pike has lots of endurance!" Les said, "Yes, they're tough fish. They have plenty of sharp teeth too. Be careful when we land it." Jeff said, "Thanks for the vote of confidence. I'll be careful. I'm glad you think I'll land it." Les reached over and tightened the drag a little on the reel, since Jeff was not familiar with it. The handle started turning harder, but the pike was starting to be pulled closer to the boat. Jeff pumped the rod just like he did when he was musky fishing. Les said, "I've been meaning to ask. How did both of you get all those blisters on your faces and hands?" Jeff said, "I was meaning to tell you about that. I made the mistake of trying to cook fish on my boat. The gas tank caught fire and we got a little toasted before we managed to jump overboard. My boat was a total loss, but a got a new one yesterday. The blisters don't hurt, they're just an embarrassment." Les said, "I never even allow smoking on my boat. You and Bill are lucky to be alive. I think God was watching after you." Bill said, "I think you're right. I'm starting to pray a lot more and think about God." Jeff and I both have been pretty bitter about treatment by our fellow humans, but at least it would appear that God loves us." Les said, "I know what you mean about people being hateful. That's why I took up this profession. I didn't want to work in factories. At least the people that I work with are trying to have fun. They usually don't act hateful while they are fishing. Sometimes there's a lot of competitiveness, but it is usually good natured." Jeff said, "I have a great dislike for competitiveness. I'm just out for the excitement of fishing. I don't need to be better than someone else." Bill said, "I'm not out to prove anything either."

Jeff let out a cry as the pike jumped close to the boat, "He's jumping. He's getting desperate. It's a good sign isn't it, Les?" Les said, "Yes, you are close to landing him now. Don't get too excited and crank too hard. Ease him into the boat. Bill, here's the net. You can net him." Bill leaned over the boat with the net as he saw the fish coming in close. He went for the head, just like he did with muskies. With great effort he hoisted the big pike into the boat. They measured the fish. It was 48 inches long. Les said, "Erma loves to eat fresh pike. Why don't we keep this one? There are plenty of them in this lake. Jeff said, "I guess it's a good idea. I usually release big fish, but I'd like to see what a pike tastes like." Bill said, "Yes, I'd like us to keep it too. But how do you clean this big of a fish?" Les said, "I'll fillet it. You'll still need to watch out for the small bones."

They took the lure out of the pike's mouth and placed it in the cooler. Its tail hung out over the edge of the cooler. Les said, "I'll speed us back to shore so the fish doesn't spoil." He powered up the boat and headed home. Jeff said, "I'd love to run a charter fishing service like this. I'm going to give it some thought. First, I want to fish for all the different types of fish that I am interested in. And I want to go to lots of remote locations to fish, places where there are only a few fishermen. Then, maybe I could specialize in a few types like you have, Les." Les said, "It's a good life. I always fish right along with my clients. It would get boring to just watch others fish." Jeff said, "I would do that too. How much does a 24 cabin cruiser cost?" Les said, "You can get a good used one for about $14,000.00. I bought this one 20 years ago for $5,000.00. They've gone up since then. The Canadian government doesn't allow much development along the lake shore. If you wanted to start a fishing charter in Canada, you'd need to buy someone else's business when they retire. Of course there are good places for a charter fishing business in plenty of locations in the States. Michigan has some of the best fishing in the world, and it's not so far from your home." Jeff said, "I like that idea. I could take people on charter trips to Lake Tippicanoe." Bill exclaimed, "You'd better get some good fire insurance first!" Jeff responded, "I wouldn't even allow smoking on the boat! I've learned my lesson!"

Bill said, "You wouldn't need a big boat for Lake Tippicanoe." Jeff said, "I wonder what size would be best? The river that leads to the lake is shallow and the muskies hang out in the shallow weedy parts of the lake." Les said, "If you plan on taking two clients with you at a time, I would think you would want at least a 16 foot aluminum boat. The aluminum boats don't sink so deeply into the water. They're lighter. 16 feet would give the clients room to move around. If you get a 19 footer, you could go out on the Great Lakes on calm days. Even the 24 footers like this one don't tackle rough weather on the Great Lakes. Most perch fishermen don't like waves much over five feet high, although some will ask me to take them out in seven foot waves. I'd prefer to have a 31 footer if I'm going to stay out on seven foot waves all day." Bill said, "I think that seven foot waves are a little too large. The bigger the boat the better. An inexperienced person feels more secure with a larger boat." Jeff said, "I think I'll just take one person with me for charter fishing in my 14 foot boat. I might buy a 24 foot boat for charter fishing on Lake Michigan." Les replied, "Yes, that sounds like the best of both worlds. A big boat for the big lake and a smaller boat for a smaller lake." Jeff went on with his pipe dreaming until their boat pulled into the channel at Les's property.

The men took the pike up to the cabin to show off to Erma. She came to the door and was visibly impressed. She said, "I'll set the table. How many perch did you catch?" Les said, "101 twelve inchers. They were biting real well until this big pike chased them away. It'll take us a couple hours to clean all these fish. We'd better get started right away if we want to get done before dark." They went out to the lake shore and cleaned the fish. Les and Jeff gutted the fish and removed fins, while Bill ran the rotary fish skinner. When they had worked for about an hour, Les took some of the fish to Erma to cook. Then he returned to help finish cleaning the fish. They finished just as the sun was setting.

The men sat around the stove and recounted the events of the day while Erma cooked the fish for supper. The fish smelled good as they cooked. Erma became very interested when she heard about the giant pike that got away. She said, "Maybe tomorrow we could go pike fishing along the beach." Les said, "We're the only ones with pike rods." Erma said, "Well, Jeff and Bill would learn what types of locations to fish. If they are really biting we could let them use our rods and reels." Les said, "What do you think, Jeff?" Jeff responded, "Well, I think it would be a good way to spend the day. How about you, Bill?" Bill said, "Sounds good to me." They all sat down to a big fish dinner. After dinner they played some more cards and then went to bed.

Early the next morning they set out for some shoreline pike fishing. They drove about 20 miles north along the shore till they came to an area of land that jutted out into the lake. Erma cast out first. The shoreline was strewn with boulders that were close together. Bill asked, "How will you get the fish in if you catch one." Les said, "You'll see. We can make it over those boulders when we have to." Suddenly the reel started to sing out as a pike began its run with the lure. Erma was losing most of the line on the reel. Les ran up and tried to tighten the drag. It was a front mounted drag, and he caught his finger in the line. This caused the pike to break off. Erma lost her temper and it wasn't a pretty sight. She was quite sore at Les. She pouted for most of the day.

Les said he would take them fishing for rainbow trout the next day. They would just call it quits for today. He would take them for an evening boat ride. They returned to the cabin and went out in the boat. They stayed out for a long time and waited for Erma to regain her normal happy attitude. When they returned she had supper ready and all bad feelings were over. They ate more perch and homemade bread with apple butter. There was some more pike too. They were getting a little tired of the small bones in the pike. Erma said, "I never get tired of pike." She ate lots of pike. The men stuffed themselves on perch.

The next morning they loaded an eight foot jon boat onto Les's car and headed for the trout lake. It was such a small lake that it wasn't even named. They had to climb for several hours to reach the lake. When they got there they discovered several log rafts that Les had made several years earlier. The rafts were somewhat waterlogged, but Jeff and Les took one of the rafts anyway. Bill took the jon boat. They fished with wax worms and red worms, using small number 12 hooks. Bill was the first to land a fish. He exclaimed, "These are beautiful fish!" He baited his hook again eagerly and started to fish. Les and Jeff caught several trout. They put them on a stringer and kept on fishing. Then disaster struck. Jeff saw a leech swimming toward Les's leg. He told Les about the leech and Les got so distracted that he fell into the lake. He couldn't swim very well, and Bill had to rescue him with the jon boat. Les couldn't make it all the way into the boat. Bill had to row to shore with Les hanging over the back end of the boat. It was a sight to see.

Les was good natured about his bad luck. They had caught seven rainbow trout that were all nice sized. The fish were about 12 inches long. Les gutted the trout and headed back to the car. They loaded the boat and drove back to the cabin. Erma cooked the trout and they all enjoyed a rare feast.

That evening Bill wrote in his journal. "I have found new meaning for life. It is the beauty that is experienced from catching a rainbow trout. The thrill of catching many nice sized perch is also great. I temporarily forgot about man's inhumanity to man. I was able to forget that I ever worked in a factory. This is the state of mind that I will strive for from now on for as long as I live. Jeff didn't complain once on this trip about people. And he is the most misanthropic person I have ever met. At first I thought he was misogynist and only hated women; but when you get to know him, you realize that he hates men and women equally. And I mean almost all men and women. How he expects to run a charter fishing service is beyond me. He hates other fishermen, with the exception of me. I'll have to think of a way to change his mind, or he will be wasting a lot of money. He can't afford a 24 foot boat unless it is making plenty of money for him from charters. I guess I'll just keep him busy taking me fishing. Then he will be too busy for charter work."

The next morning Jeff and Bill waved goodbye to Les and Erma and drove back to New Paris. They were glad to see their wives. Each went to his own home and made passionate love to his wife. They did "honey do lists" and then got together for some Miller and planned the next fishing trip. Bill said, "What would you recommend for our next fishing expedition, Jeff?" Jeff answered, "I'd like to go to Baja Mexico. I read that there is a place called Loreto where you can fish for four days at a cost of only $435.00. Room, food, beer, boat and guide are included. You have to buy your own bait and air fare. The air fare is $600.00 each, round trip. I think we might want to drive. We have plenty of time, and it would save us several hundred dollars." Bill responded, "I need to save all the money I can. Let's drive. We can live on bread and water. That will help us keep the cost down." Jeff said, "I can do it if you can. By the way, the guides at Loreto don't speak much English and about all they do is steer the boat. They can buy live bait for you, but you are on your own to find a fishing technique that works. I bought a book last week on the subject. It includes saltwater baits and has pictures of all the different types of salt water fish. We can take the book with us. We'll point to the fish that we want to fish for. The guides will know where that kind of fish are." Bill said, "It sounds like a good plan. Let's ask our wives what they think about it." Jeff said, "I'll call you after supper to find out what your wife said. I know my wife won't mind. We'll be gone about two weeks."

Bill went home and told Sandy his plan. She was delighted for him. She said, "This will give you more to write about. Maybe you'll even get a story about Mexico published someday. I'll pack lots of food so you can save money on the trip." Bill said, "We are just going to have bread and water. We are very serious about saving money." Sandy said, "It's alright with me, but you must promise to take your vitamins. Bread alone isn't a very healthy diet. At least you won't get sick from meat that has sat around too long unrefrigerated. I've heard that there are problems with that in Mexico. You can get sick off the water there too. I want you to promise me that you will only drink beer in Mexico." Bill said, "I promise." They went to the bedroom together and packed some clothes for the trip.

At Jeff's house they were packing too. Jeff's wife thought of the same thing Sandy had thought of. She said, "Don't get sick on the water, Jeff. Promise me that you will only drink beer in Mexico." Jeff said, "Alright dear, if you insist. I will only drink beer." Nancy said, "It is good to only eat bread. It will help you remember that you must be conservative with your spending. She gave him a kiss on the lips and said, "I want you to send me a post card or two." Jeff said, "I'll send you one every day. I need to go over to Bill's to see if he can go on the trip."

Jeff walked across the street to Bill's house and knocked on the door. Bill answered the door and said, "The trip is on. Only we have to promise to drink only beer in Mexico. No water allowed." Jeff said, "My wife thought of the same thing." Bill said, "Can you come in for awhile?" Jeff answered, "No, I have to find my passport. Have you got yours?" Bill replied, "Yes, I have it in my camera bag. When are we leaving?" Jeff answered, "I'd like to leave in about an hour. We can make better time if we drive at night. There won't be so much traffic." Bill said, "I can be ready in an hour. I'll meet you at your place." Both men spent the hour finishing with packing and saying goodbye to their wives.

CHAPTER THREE

The Baja Experience

At 8:00 o'clock in the evening they headed for the Baja Peninsula. They took the Saturn. Bill drove first. He stayed about five m.p.h. above the speed limit. They listened to Big Band music as they drove. Jeff read the road map and kept Bill informed about where to turn and which roads to take. They made good time. By 11:00 o'clock the next morning, they were in Arizona. They had traded off driving every couple hours. When Jeff drove, he insisted on going close to 100 m.p.h. He couldn't wait to get to Loreto.

It was Sunday afternoon when they reached the Mexican border in southern California. They got on highway "1" and followed it all the way to Loreto. They arrived around supper time on Monday. There had been no problems in getting across the border. They went right to the beach and ask directions to the fishing charters. People were helpful, and both men spoke enough Spanish that they were able to find the place quickly. They paid for the charter and agreed that they would go out fishing the next morning at 6:00 o'clock. They gave the guide some money for live bait. His name was Carlos. He was about 60 years old, short, and had white hair and moustache. He wore all white clothes and a white hat. He encouraged them to buy hats. He said, "El sol hace mucho calor." Jeff said, "That means that the sun gets very hot. We'd better take his advice." Bill said, "Donde es bueno a comprar un sombrero?" The guide pointed to a shop across the street. The men went into the shop and each bought a sombrero. Jeff didn't have any Mexican money yet, so he just started counting out one dollar bills until the girl at the counter said enough and gave him the change. They went back to the charter office and were shown to their room, which was overlooking the Sea of Cortez. It was a modern room with air conditioning and a stove and refrigerator. When Bill opened the refrigerator, he found that it was stocked with Corona, a premium Mexican beer. He asked Jeff, "Are you thirsty? We have plenty of beer." Jeff said, "I'll take one. Then I need to go back to that shop and get some post cards. I need to send a card to my wife." They drank a beer and then went back to the shop.

The girl behind the counter appeared to be about 19 years old. She had pretty long black hair and dark brown eyes. Her skin was well tanned from much time spent on the beach. She was slender yet well proportioned. She wore a deep plunging blouse that showed off her wonderful figure. Jeff and Bill each picked out a dozen post cards of the beach and fishing scenes. Jeff paid for all of them with one dollar. He gave the girl a quarter tip. She thanked him and said, "Your guide often drinks too much. He rarely gets up till around noon. He is a good fisherman, but you will have to wait till the afternoon to fish with him. I can take you out in the morning. I have a girl friend who can help me. We are very good fishermen. All you have to do is let us keep the fish and give us some tips if you think we are doing a good job. My name is Anita and my friend's name is Juanita." Jeff said, "I guess it wouldn't hurt to buy some insurance. We really want to fish in the morning before it gets hot. Meet us at the pier at 6:00 o'clock. Your English is very good." She said, "Thank you. You can pay me later for the bait. I know that you already paid Carlos for the bait. My girlfriend speaks English. We often help Carlos with his charters. He likes to sleep in." Jeff said, "Thanks for the help. I'm looking forward to fishing with you."

He and Bill went back to the room and wrote post cards. They heard a knock on the door and Bill went to open it. It was a beautiful girl who was pushing a cart full of food. They tipped her and she asked, "Is there anything else that you would like. I can get you anything. Anything at all." Bill said, "We would like some postage stamps. And then please take these post cards to the mail box." She said, "I will get the stamps right away." She left for a few minutes and then returned with the stamps. She said, "I can stay and talk for a little while if you like. She was about 20 years old and was very shapely. Her eyes were playful. She obviously liked them. Jeff said, "Please sit with us for awhile. We would like to get information about the area." She sat close to Jeff and pulled her skirt up a little to show off her beautiful legs. She said, "I am the owner's daughter. He likes for me to make the customers feel at home. My name is Maria. You can call the front desk and ask for me at any time. I live right next door. I'll be glad to help keep you both informed about things.

She leaned down to rub her ankle and Jeff had a wonderful view of her exquisite chest. Her nipples were small and dark brown. He thought she was exceedingly attractive. She stayed through the meal and helped them open the crab legs and lobster. Jeff said, "What is your last name, Maria? She said, "It is Gomez. My father is Juan Gomez. He is a prominent man in this city. The fishing tourism is going well here. I hope you will tell your friends how well we treat our customers." Jeff said, "I will be sure to tell everyone how much fun it is here." She went over behind Bill and started massaging his neck and shoulders. She said, "I give free back rubs to special customers such as yourselves. You must both have sore muscles from such a long drive. I like your car. It is very sleek and stylish." After she had rubbed both of there necks she said, "I don't want you to think that I am coming on to you. I only give back rubs. My father is very strict. He doesn't allow me to be sexual with our clients. He says that I must stay pure, so that a respectable man will want to marry me." Bill said, "We want you to stay respectable. I think I can speak for Jeff when I say that it would be fine for you to come back at 9:00 for our back rubs. We want to get to bed early so we can fish in the morning." Maria said, "I will be here at 9:00 o'clock.

When Maria returned, she was dressed in a plush white bath robe. She lit a candle and turned off the other lights. She said, "I want you each to remove your clothes and lay on your stomach in your bed. You can trust me to be professional. I only want to give you pleasure and at the same time stay pure for my future husband. She watched intently as they disrobed. She went to Bill first and spread some oil on his back. She rubbed and patted for a long time. Then she went to Jeff and rubbed his back. She gave a very professional back rub. She said, "I can stay and talk for awhile if you would like, or I could dance for you. I am taking dance lessons." Jeff said, "Please dance for us. That will be wonderful." She started to dance smoothly around the room. Then she surprised them by slipping out of her robe. She was dancing nude for them now. They didn't want to interrupt her out of respect for her art. When she had danced for 20 minutes she finally stopped and put her robe back on.

Bill said, "You are a beautiful woman and you dance very well." He didn't want to be the one to tell her that she should keep her clothes on with them." Jeff said, "Maria. We are married men and don't want to lust for other women too much. I'll have to ask you to keep your clothes on after this. Your dancing was wonderful. It will be just as pleasing if you keep your clothes on. Please come again tomorrow night and dance again for us. Now we need to get our sleep. Please wake us at 6:00 o'clock tomorrow morning.

In the morning Maria woke them at 6:00 o'clock. She smiled and said, "I'm looking forward to tonight." It is pleasing to me that you will allow further back rubs. I truly enjoy being pleasurable to powerful men such as yourselves. Your muscles are so pronounced. I love to work them over with my hands. The oil feels so nice on your skin. I have a new dance planned for both of you." Maria pushed her breakfast cart into the room and passed them their meal of eggs, bacon and toast. She let her robe fall open so that they could watch her breasts while they ate. They enjoyed the view. After they had finished eating, she took the cart away. They laughed and looked at each other. Jeff said,

"This certainly is the royal treatment. I wonder what the rest of the girls are like here." Bill said, "I'm looking forward to finding out. They got dressed and went to the pier.

Anita and her friend were waiting at the boat, which they called a ponga. Anita introduced her friend, "This is Juanita. Juanita this is Bill and this is Jeff. They are from the States." Juanita shook their hands and said, "I hope you don't mind if we sun bath while we guide you in fishing. We don't get much time to keep our tans in shape." Jeff said, "We don't mind. We are pretty self sufficient about fishing. Did you bring the live bait?" Anita said, "Yes, we have plenty. I brought a couple heavy rods and reels for you to rent. They are reasonable. Most tourists don't own the heavy equipment that is needed for some of our heavier fish." Jeff said, "That was thoughtful. How much are they?" She said, "Only two dollars total." Jeff handed her the two dollars and said, "That is a nice price. You are taking good care of us." She said, "Thank you. I intend to take very good care of you." She loaded the equipment onto the ponga and they motored out to sea. They headed north and east. Jeff said, "What is your last name Anita?" Anita said, "Fernandez, Anita Fernandez." Jeff said, "What is your last name, Juanita?" Juanita said, "Rojas, Juanita Rojas." Jeff said, "Those are fine names. I will remember them." After they were out of sight from the city, Anita and Juanita took off some clothing to reveal the white bikinis they were wearing. They were both shapely young women without an ounce of fat on them. They could have been models for magazines.

Anita asked Jeff to oil her body. He obliged only too willingly. Bill oiled up Juanita. He took his time, and looked her body over carefully. He said, "You are an attractive woman Juanita. Do you have a boy friend?" She said, "Sometimes I date, but I am not going steady. I am still a virgin. My family insists that I stay pure till I am married." Bill said, "That sounds familiar. It must be a general custom here." Anita said, "I am a virgin too. All women from Loreto want to stay virgins and marry a nice man. It is terrible when some lose their virginity and fall into disgrace. It is a great embarrassment to their family." Juanita said, "Anita said that I could trust both of you. I want to get a nice tan so . . ." She dropped off the top of her swim suit. Juanita dropped off hers too. Jeff and Bill were surprised. Jeff said, "Please girls! Don't go crazy. You can't be topless here on the boat with us! He and Bill deftly helped the girls get their tops back on.

The girls looked a little disappointed, but they cheered up right away and became talkative. Anita motored the boat to the north and east, away from the city. When they were barely in site of Loreto, she stopped and asked Juanita, "Will you drop the drift anchor overboard. It's too deep here for the lead anchor. We don't have enough rope." Juanita said, "I've got it. You don't have to help me." She threw the parachute like, drift anchor overboard. She said, "There's hardly any wind. We won't drift much today." Jeff said, "Do you think there are fish here?" Anita said, "There are fish anywhere in the Sea of Cortez. I mainly wanted to get out of sight from the city. I don't like people watching me. When grown men are with women alone on the sea, you never know what will happen." She giggled coyly. Jeff said, "Well, we came to fish, not to get into trouble with young girls." Anita said, "I am not young. I'm nineteen years old. Then she whispered in Jeff's ear. We want to really deserve our guide tips. We want to give the presidential treatment. Your President of the United States always got special treatment from that female aid of his. She gave him what you Americans call the 'blew job'. We want to give that same presidential treatment. You are honored guests in our country." Jeff whispered back, "You mean to say 'oral s-x'. Our President was a little different. Not all Americans are that way. Right now, we just want to fish. You can keep the bait alive and bring us a beer when we ask for it. That's all we need." Juanita said, "I can do that." She smiled and went for the bait. She put some fresh water on them and fished out a nice one for Bill. Bill said, "Jeff, how do you bait a hook for salt water fish. What are we fishing for? How deep are they?" Jeff said, "Anita, you said you were a fisherman. What are we fishing for?" Anita said, "Most people start with red snapper. They are excellent eating fish and they are found at different depths. I'd try the bottom first. It's about 600 feet deep here. I will bait the hooks." She buried the big hook into the flesh of a six inch mullet, and threw it overboard. There was a one ounce lead weight on the line, and it went quickly to the bottom of the sea.

Next, she baited Jeff's line and threw it overboard. She said, "See how professional I can be?" Jeff said, "Good work Anita. Can one of you get us each a beer? You can each drink one too if you want. Just don't drink too many. We need you to get us back to Loreto in one piece." Anita grabbed a beer and brought it to Jeff. Juanita got one for Bill. Then they each opened a beer and drank with the men.

After about an hour Jeff said, "I thought you said there were fish everywhere in the Sea of Cortez." Anita said, "Try different depths now. Slowly bring your bait up from the bottom and see if something takes the bait." Jeff and Bill followed her advice. Bill got a bite and started to reel. Anita said, "Keep track of how many times you turn the handle. That will tell you how deep the fish was. You can go back to that same depth and catch another fish." Bill counted the turns of the crank. The fish came to the surface and Bill said, "300 cranks." Anita said, "That's a red snapper. They usually travel in schools. We may catch lots of them. I'll bait your hook again so you can get another one. Do you know how many inches each turn of your reel's crank is?" Jeff said, "It's 12 inches." Anita said, "Then the fish are 300 feet down." She threw the bait overboard and then went to sit at Jeff's feet and watch him fish. She held onto his leg and leaned against it. Jeff didn't mind. He thought she was funny. Like a little kitten that wanted affection.

Juanita sat at Bill's feet and played with his bare feet. He said, "Careful. I'm ticklish. I don't want to drop my rod into the sea." She stopped tickling and leaned against his legs, watching his line in the water. The fish started biting again in about 20 minutes. Jeff and Bill pulled up about 30 large red snappers that weighed about six pounds each. The cooler was getting full of fish. Luckily the girls had brought plenty of ice. The cooler was large enough to hold beer, fish and ice.

Jeff said, "What other fish are there to catch?" Anita said, "I brought some squid to use for bait to catch grouper. They are sometimes quite big and strong, so you'd better use the heavy rods and reels that I brought." She jumped up and grabbed a rod and handed it to Jeff. Then she baited his hook with the squid. She hid most of the hook in the squid's flesh. She didn't mind the slimy squid's feel on her hands at all. Jeff decided that she was a good fisherman. He almost forgot for a moment that she was in a skimpy bikini. He was having a good time. Jeff said, "Are you having a good time, Bill?" Bill said, "I'm having a great time. I think I'll just keep catching these red snappers." Jeff said, "That's fine. I'm going to catch a grouper. How big do they get, Anita?" Anita said, "I'm not sure how big they get. I've seen one that weighed 80 pounds." Jeff said, "One that big would be fun to catch. I'd settle for 20 pounds." He started fishing. Anita sat at his feet and caressed his leg. It felt good and Jeff didn't complain.

After about an hour Jeff hooked a nice sized fish. It pulled the boat noticeably as he reeled it in. He had to pump the rod. It was difficult to bring the fish up from the bottom. He pulled the rod up to the 12:00 o'clock position, and then cranked rapidly down to the 3:00 o'clock position. He worked on the fish for quite awhile. Finally, the fish surfaced and Anita netted it. Jeff helped her heave it onto the boat. It weighted 40 pounds. Jeff had Anita took a picture of him with the fish. Bill kept catching red snapper. After several hours, he had brought their total up to 45 fish plus the grouper. Jeff ordered another round of beer for everyone. The girls eagerly opened the bottles and served them. It was a little past noon and everyone was starting to feel the heat. The sky was clear and the sun was beating down mercilessly. Bill said, "Why don't we go back to the room till around 4:00 o'clock and then fish for awhile with Carlos if we can find him." Jeff said, "That sounds good. We can fish with the girls again in the morning." They reeled in their lines and Anita said, "Juanita, bring in the anchor." Juanita did as she was told. Anita started the motor and steered them back to Loreto.

Carlos was sitting on the pier waiting for them. He was sleeping at the far end of the pier. Jeff went up to him and shook his shoulder. He woke and said, "Mr. Mullet. Will I be taking you fishing today?" Jeff said, "Yes, we would like to have you take us out for grouper and red snapper at 4:00 o'clock this afternoon. We have plenty of bait left from this morning. Keep the bait fresh for us, will you?" Carlos said, "I will be glad too." He helped the girls tie the boat to the pier. The girls said, "We will take the fish to the poor people in Loreto." Jeff gave them each a five dollar tip. He said, "Will you girls meet us as 6:00 in the morning for more fishing?" Anita said, "We will be here. Can we come to your room this evening to play some cards?" Jeff said, "That will be fine. We have no other plans." The girls giggled and ran off with the fish.

Bill said, "What do you think they have planned this time?" Jeff said, "I think they are just bored. This is the start of the season and they haven't seen any Americans this year, probably." Carlos said, "You are right. You two are the first Americans this year. The girls have been anticipating the arrival of tourists. It is interesting to them." Jeff said, "Carlos, you must come to the motel and have a drink with us. It is too hot to fish right now." Carlos said, "I will have one drink. I will stop at one. I drank too much last night. That is why the girls always take the morning charter. I can't wake up in time. Sorry I was late." Jeff said, "We truly enjoyed being with the girls. Don't apologize. They made our trip memorable." Carlos said, "I have a feeling that they may be planning to try to make your trip even more memorable. They say that they are virgins, but it is as I think you Americans say, a technical virginity. They would like to smother both of you with their furry little female parts."

Jeff said, "Thanks for the warning Carlos. I was starting to wonder about that virginity story. It made them seem very attractive." Bill said, "They seemed a little less than innocent. We'll watch out for them." Carlos asked, "What card games do you know?" Jeff said, "We know hearts, rook and a little poker." Carlos said, "They'll want to play strip poker. Then they'll lose on purpose. I used to listen in at the window." Jeff said, "Thanks for the warning. We'll make them play hearts. Come with us now and we'll have that drink I spoke of." They all went over to the motel and rang for room service. Maria answered and took their order for three beers. She brought them immediately. Carlos tipped her and gave her a wink. She smiled to him knowingly and then looked at Jeff and Bill. She smiled big and said, "Don't let Carlos tell big stories about me. If he does, please keep them to yourselves. I have to keep my job you know." Then she left them. Carlos said, "She thinks that I will tell you that I have been having an affair with her. She likes to pet me. She thinks I am a kitten I guess." Then he laughed. "I enjoy her attentions, but I don't know if it will ever amount to anything. After all, I am much older than she is. I'm 60 years old."

They finished their drinks and then let Carlos take them on a tour of the blocks that surrounded the motel. Their motel was named El Pesca Grande. There was a neon sign over the main entrance. Carlos said, "Notice the main landmarks as you move around town. Many of the streets aren't named. It's easy to get lost. I don't move real fast, so you should be able to stay with me. They walked to the north and found a store that had camera film. Jeff always noted things like that, even though he had brought plenty of film. They stopped at a small store front where there was dipped ice cream. Carlos said, "I recommend the coffee flavored ice cream. The flavor is delicious." Bill and Jeff ordered three coffee flavored cones. They weren't disappointed. Bill said, "This is the best ice cream I have ever had!" Jeff said, "I agree. This is excellent ice cream." They walked a little further and then turned right. They walked a couple blocks till they reached the public beach.

They walked along the coast several hundred yards and admired the young women on the beach in their bikinis. Carlos said, "Even though I am old, I never tire of watching the girls in the bikinis. They look so young and healthy. It causes my blood to circulate better." Jeff said, "There are some beautiful women in this town. They aren't as fat as most people in the States. We are all over fed. We eat the wrong kinds of food and we don't get enough exercise."

Carlos said, "I like to come here with my camera. It has a telephoto lens. Several years ago a customer gave it to me to pay for his fishing. He wanted to stay a couple more days, and was running out of cash. Film is expensive here, so I order my film on the internet. Maria helps me run the computer. She has one in her room at the motel. Her father lets her stay there, since she argues with him when she is at home." Once in awhile some of the girls will show me their breasts for the camera. The film never gets developed though. It is frustrating. Someday I would like to have a digital camera and computer. Then I could keep pictures of the girls when they show their chests. They are so attractive. I feel younger when they do that. They love to make me feel young." Jeff said, "When the price of those cameras comes down, I'll bring you one. Computers are already inexpensive. Your dream is not out of your reach." They sat for awhile and watched the girls. Soon two of them were flashing the men. They were about 18 years old. The girls were both slender and well developed. Their breasts were pale colored and obviously needed more sun. The men watched the black haired beauties with appreciation. The girls giggled and then got up and ran away.

The men walked on down the beach to the south until they came to the motel. It was getting to be close to 4:00 o'clock, so they went to the pier and helped Carlos launch the panga. They road the boat for about 20 minutes. Carlos took them south of Loreto several miles. They stopped over a shallow spot surrounded by deeper water. Carlos said, "The fish like these shallow spots. There is food for them here." He baited the lines with mullet and threw them in the water. Jeff and Bill manned the poles. Red snapper started biting right away. They caught twenty in about an hour. The fish averaged around 10 pounds each. Jeff said, "These are bigger than the ones we caught with the girls." Carlos said, "I keep this spot a secret. It took me years to find it. Why should I let others use it who aren't paying me?" Jeff said, "That's a good point. Carlos said, "That is the limit for today. We can catch and release till sunset if you like." Bill said, "The girls had us catch 40 or more fish to keep. Why the difference?" Carlos said, "The girls don't care about the law. They think the conservation officer won't fine them. They are wrong. I hope, for their sake, they don't get caught. The fish are for a good cause; to feed poor people. But, taking that many fish is illegal. I don't want to lose my license." Bill said, "What shall we do tomorrow? The girls will want us to take fish over the limit." Carlos said, "Do what you want to do. The fine isn't too high for red snapper. They mainly fine people for lobster and shrimp. That's where the money is."

As Carlos baited the lines, Bill noticed that his fingers were quite thick and strong looking. There were cracks in the skin on his fingers. He was quite skilled at baiting hooks. His hands moved quickly and carefully. Bill said, "Do you ever hook yourself when you bait the fish?" Carlos laughed and said, "The minute that I feel the point of the hook I stop. It would not be wise to stick the hook into my hand. I am not that clumsy." Then he chuckled some more and said, "I get hooked by women often, though. Maria can catch me any time she wants me. I told her that I am getting old. She mustn't pet me more than twice a week during the tourist season. If she does, I won't have the energy to take the fishermen out in the afternoon." She agreed, but during the off season she pets me every other night. She doesn't trust younger men. She worries that a younger man might rape her. She doesn't want to have children. She says that she is too young for that. It would ruin her figure."

Bill said, "It must be rough trying to keep up with a young woman like her. Don't you get jealous when she is with other men?" Carlos said, "I think that she just gives backrubs and dances naked. She is not my wife. Why should I complain? She is just a friend; a friend who is quite unusual." Bill said, "Unusual is right. She knows how to make men long for her, but I will try to resist. I would feel embarrassed around you, Carlos, if I had her."

Carlos said, "She always comes to me out on the pier around 2:00 o'clock in the morning. No one else is awake then. She wears a thick terry cloth robe. That is all she has on. I hear the robe drop on the pier and then the fun begins. She really knows how to give pleasure. If it wasn't for her skill, I wouldn't be able to respond so often at my age. Jeff said, "I wish my wife was like that. For her, it's like a duty. She only gets excited when I stimulate her." Bill said, "My wife is a little the same. She doesn't have an intense longing for sex. I often have to talk her into it. I wonder why only certain women are that way." Jeff said, "I think that some women have high hormone levels. If they have lots of estrogen, they long for sex more than other women. Carlos said, "I think it is more complicated than that. Some women get the most enjoyment by seeing themselves as very exciting to men. Some men's wives take them for granted and just want to do the minimum thing that will satisfy their man. These lazy women often lose their men to women such as Maria. She is quite a big temptation to such men. I am surprised that you two have resisted."

Jeff said, "Well, the week isn't over yet. I'm not going to start bragging yet. She is terribly tempting. I'd like to take a shower with a woman like her. I mean I bet some men would like to get in the shower with her." Bill laughed, "Yeah, it's good that you corrected that. I agree. Some men would like to be in the shower with Maria." Then he chuckled. They caught and released some more fish. The sun was starting to get low in the sky. Carlos said, "I think we might want to go back now. It is easier to dock the boat when there is still some daylight left. We can do some night fishing if you like. There is little wind and the sky is clear. The stars would be nice to watch. We could bring Maria, Anita and Juanita out. They could bait our hooks with flashlights. I don't allow gas lanterns on the boat. It is a fire hazard." Jeff and Bill looked at each other. Jeff said, "We know about fires on boats. We don't like cooking on a boat either."

Carlos said, "I noticed the blisters on your faces and hands. They are healing nicely." Jeff said, "We set our boat on fire a week ago. The boat was a total loss. We were trying to cook some fish on the boat. The gas line must have had a leak in it." Carlos said, "That is bad luck. How will you fish now?" Jeff said, "I bought a new boat the next day. Now I have to control my spending so that I don't have to go back to work in the factories. I'm too old for that, and I don't enjoy it. I want to fish for the rest of my life." Carlos said, "I will give you both a discount if you come here every year. Half price. That's only about $100 for each of you. Promise me you will come." Jeff said, "We are having a great time. It is flattering to have beautiful young women trying to get in your pants all the time. And the fishing is great. I think you can count on us to return every year. For that price we will come back every three months." Bill said, "I agree. I'm having the most wonderful time of my life. I love the attention of the girls, and I'm learning to be a skilled fisherman."

Carlos said, "Shall we fish tonight then, and bring the girls?" Jeff said, "Yes, let's do it. We will need plenty of beer. Carlos roared the white 22ft. panga back to the dock. They tied up the boat, and Carlos went to get the girls. In about ten minutes Juanita and Anita came giggling and whispering something about the presidential treatment. Maria was wheeling a wheelbarrow full of beer and food. She said, "You men know how to live. Carlos doesn't take many fishermen out at night. You must be paying him well." Jeff said, "He wants to see the stars from out on the sea. We aren't paying him any extra. We did agree to come here every three months if we can come for half price." Maria said, "That's a bargain for you and more business for us. Both of us win. A wonderful arrangement!" Carlos steered the panga slowly through the small waves as they went straight out to sea. They moved east and watched to the west as the last bit of red disappeared from the sunset. After they had gone east for about 20 minutes, Carlos cut the motor. The girls opened the cooler and passed out beer and sandwiches. The girls were all dressed in white bikinis. They looked similar in many ways. Their bodies were brown and slender. They had long black hair. Maria had a slightly more curvatious body than Anita and Juanita. She wore her bikini a little lower on her hips. Juanita had a distinguishing mole on her left cheek, not far from her mouth. Anita's hair line was a little higher than Juanita's. Juanita had more curve to her butt than Anita and she had slightly larger breasts. All the women had dark brown eyes, except that Maria's had a slight tint of green to them.

After they had all eaten, the girls started to bait hooks. Maria didn't have much experience at that, so she just passed the bait to the other girls and let them put the bait on the hook. Soon all the hooks were baited and in the water. Jeff explained to the girls, "We would like all of you to drink a beer every time we do. That way you will seem more like one of us. We will feel more at home." Anita said, "I will be glad to! I want to be one of you." Juanita said, "I will drink gladly with my friends." Maria said, "I want you to feel at home. I will drink with you gladly." They all opened another beer.

Maria said, "In Mexico we call a beer, cervesa." Jeff said, "Cervesa. I'll remember that word. It's an important word." They all finished a beer and another round was brought out. Jeff said, "In America we say, 'What is good for the goose is good for the gander.' It means that what is good for one person is good for another." Maria repeated the phrase, "What is good for the goose is good for the gander. That is an interesting saying. Why do you mention it now?" Jeff said, "When I have a beer you have a beer. It is the same thing." She said, "Oh, now I see. Don't worry, I will keep up with you. I have what you Americans refer to as 'the bottomless pit'. I think that means that I can drink a lot of beer." Jeff said, "You are right. You remember well." He said, "Cervesa." Maria said, "You remember well also."

Juanita and Anita were giving Carlos and Bill backrubs. They had removed the men's shirts and had them covered with oil. Juanita and Anita were chattering in rapid Spanish as they rubbed the men's backs. Maria scolded them. "Speak in English so Bill can understand you. Do you want him to feel left out?" Anita said, "Yes, you are right. We will speak English. Bill you have a very nice butt. And you too Carlos." They both giggled and continued to rub the men's backs. Carlos said, "Another round of beer, please." The girls jumped to the cooler. They stumbled a little, since they were getting drunk.

They handed another beer to everyone. Then they returned to rubbing the backs.

Maria said, "I have never gotten drunk with a man before. You must promise to be a gentleman." She giggled. Jeff said, "I will be a gentleman with you, because I think you belong to Carlos. The other girls may be a different situation." Maria said, "You are right. They like you. I don't think they want you to be a gentleman. It is difficult to work at a resort and not let the men have you? They are so flattering, and they want to buy you lots of drinks." Jeff said, "Carlos told us that you do things to him in his sleep." Maria said, "I don't care that you know. I just long for him. He is old enough to resist going all the way. I don't want babies." Jeff said, "I understand. I think it is wonderful that you can give so much pleasure to an older man." Maria said, "If he could, I would have him every night. He is so powerful. He is still very much a man. I love to give him pleasure. It excites me. He pretends to be asleep. I know he is awake. I stand before him in the moon light so that he can see my whole body. I love for him to see me. He peeks out from the slits of his eyes. He pretends to be asleep." Jeff said, "I could use another beer, please." Maria said, "So could I. I really talk up a storm when I'm drunk." She stumbled over to the cooler and got a couple more beer. She reeled in the fishing lines, since no one seemed interested in fishing at the moment.

Juanita and Anita were still rubbing backs at the front of the boat. Jeff went over and traded places with Carlos so that he could be with Maria. Juanita took off Jeff's shirt and put some oil on his back. She rubbed him vigorously. She whispered in his ear. "I would like to rub your back with my bare breasts. I think it would be O.K. if you don't look, right?" Jeff said, "If it makes you happy, I will allow it. She eagerly took off her top and glided her firm breasts over his back. Anita did the same to Bill. Juanita said, "Your belt hurts my breasts, can I remove it? Jeff said, "I don't mind." Juanita took off Jeff's belt. Anita took off Bill's belt also. Juanita said, "I'd like to massage your bare butt with my breasts. Is it O.K.?" Jeff said, "I guess I could allow that. Since it's you. I don't usually permit things like that." She removed his pants and started rubbing his butt with her breasts. He could feel her trembling a little with excitement. Anita was doing the same thing to Bill.

Maria came and threw a blanket over each couple and said, "Now you can have the back rub in privacy. She giggled and went back to be with Carlos. The girls were under the blankets for several hours with Jeff and Bill. The blankets kept moving around a lot. The girls were being quite seductive, but at the same time they were keeping their virginity.

After several hours Juanita said, "Don't you both want to fish some more. After all, you came to fish." Bill said, "Yes, let's catch some more fish." The men fished while the women waited on them topless. The moonlight was bright enough that their young firm breasts could be seen clearly. Jeff said, "There is nothing better than breasts and fishing." The girls giggled and surrounded him. They all pressed their breasts up into his face. He said, "I must be in heaven." Then he got a bite, and started to reel in a large grouper. He struggled for 30 minutes to bring the big fish up from the bottom. Since Jeff was busy, the girls started smothering Bill with their breasts. When Jeff asked him to get the net, he forced himself to leave the girls. He grabbed the net and looked for the fish. Carlos held a flashlight. Soon Bill could see the monstrous grouper sticking its nose out of the water. He deftly slid the net over the head of the fish and pulled up hard with the handle. Jeff helped him lift the fish into the boat.

They weighed the fish on a hand held scales. It weighed in at 80 pounds. Anita said, "That one will feed ten families tomorrow." Jeff said, "Let's catch some more. We can feed the whole town of Loreto." Anita baited the hook and cast if overboard. In about 20 minutes both Jeff and Bill got bites at the same time. They went to opposite ends of the boat so they wouldn't get their lines tangled. Jeff said, "This fish must be even bigger than the last one!" He tightened the drag a little. His fishing rod bent almost into the water, as he reeled in line, a little at a time. Bill said, "If I land this fish, it will be the biggest I have ever caught!" He pulled up hard on the rod and then lowered quickly, reeling determinedly and with much speed. He was a natural at fishing. Bill said, "This is fun. I don't know why I never started fishing earlier in my life."

After about 40 minutes Jeff brought up his fish. Carlos netted the fish for him. It was another large grouper. Next, Bill brought up his fish. It was a grouper too. After weighing the fish, they found that Jeff's fish weighed 90 pounds and Bill's weighed 96 pounds. Carlos said, "This is probably enough grouper for one night. Why don't we try for some flounder?" Bill said, "What's a flounder?" Carlos said, "They are flat fish that live on the bottom. Some of them weigh as much as 700 pounds. Around here they get as big as 400 pounds. They are excellent for eating. I will get out the heavier rods and reels." Jeff said, "I would love t o catch one of those giant flounder." Bill said, "So would I."

While they waited on Carlos to bring the rods and reels, they watched the topless girls in the moonlight. In a few minutes Carlos returned with the rods and reels. The lines were thrown overboard and Jeff and Bill each manned a rod. They let the bait go clear to the bottom. It was an hour later when the squid bait was taken on Bill's rod. He reeled line in as fast as he could. The cranking was difficult. He would get in about 200 feet of line and then the big fish would turn and pull the line back out. It was a two hour struggle before Bill knew that the fish was close to the surface. His reel was nearly full of line now. He could feel Juanita standing behind him with her breasts against his back. He thought, "This trip is too good to be true." In a couple more minutes the fish was churning up the surface with its large fins and tail. Carlos gaffed the fish and the girls helped him haul the huge fish onto the deck. Carlos said, "This fish will have to be weighed at the fish market. Our scale isn't large enough. I know it must weigh at least 300 pounds." Bill said, "It felt like it weighed 1000 pounds!" Juanita whispered in Bill's ear, "Let's have some more fun under the blanket." Bill said, "I think that's an excellent idea. I've caught enough fish for one night." Juanita said, "I hope I am doing what you want me too. I want to stay a virgin, but we can still have plenty of fun." She giggled and pulled him under the blanket again with her. They stayed there for several hours

Finally Jeff got a bite. He started to reel in the fish. It bent his pole clear down into the water. The fish only gave up line grudgingly. It took two hours to reel in most of the line. It was a tug of war. The fish would come in several hundred feet, and then turn and take out 400 feet of line. Anita rubbed his back and arms while he worked on the fish. After another hour the flounder came to the surface. Carlos gaffed it, and Jeff and Anita helped him get the fish on the deck. It was even bigger than the last fish. Carlos said, "This one probably weighs close to 400 pounds. It was all we could do to get it onto the boat." The three couples settled into each others arms and rested till sunrise.

At sunrise, Carlos awoke. He woke up everyone and said, "We need to get the fish back to the market before they spoil. There is time though for a swim. Can all of you swim?" Jeff said, "Bill and I can swim. Can you swim, Anita?" Anita said, "Yes, I can swim and so can Juanita and Maria. We swim every day here in Loreto." Carlos said, "I will put the ladder onto the side of the boat. I have several bars of soap if anyone wants them." He lowered the ladder and climbed into the water with Maria. Jeff climbed in with Anita, and Bill climbed in with Juanita. They all played in the water and washed themselves. They were all naked and Jeff said, "This looks like a skinny dipping party. We'd better get our clothes on before other boats start coming out." Carlos said, "They are used to strange things here at Loreto. Many tourists like to skinny dip from their boats. The women like to get all around tans, and the men like to watch them." Bill said, "Do people like to have water fights here?" He splashed water at Maria. She splashed back. In seconds, everyone was splashing everyone else. Finally Jeff said, "We'd better get our fish to the market to weigh them. Bill and I can help the girls carry the fish to the poor people." Juanita said, "I think they might be embarrassed to have you see them accept free food. We will tell them about the big fish and they will come to the market to take what they can carry." Jeff said, "What ever you think is best. Bill and I can get some sleep today. I'd like to fish for blue marlin tomorrow when we are rested." Juanita said, "We don't usually keep the marlin. They are what attract many of the tourist fishermen here. We like them to be plentiful." Carlos said, "We should release them when we catch them." Jeff said, "That's fine. We will release them. Bill and I will sleep this morning and afternoon. In the evening we should all get together for a meal and fire on the beach." Maria said, "That's a great idea. The weather is supposed to be nice all week. It's a good time for supper on the beach. We can have one of the cooks prepare some of the fish we caught on an open fire. I will arrange it." Bill said, "Won't that cost extra?" Maria said, "No there is no charge. I wanted to tell you before, without sounding like bragging. My father gave me the motel last week. I am his only child and he wants me to stay in Loreto. He gave me the motel so that I will have a regular income. It pretty much runs itself. I have trustworthy and reliable workers who do everything. I will just keep track of some of the paperwork."

Jeff said, "That's amazing. I never would have dreamed that you own the motel." Maria said, "My father is usually tight fisted with his money, but he loves me and doesn't want me to leave here." Jeff said, "I can understand that." Maria said, "The money won't change the way I relate to anyone. It's just nice that I don't have to ask my father every time I need money. I don't have to worry about getting tips from the tourists." Anita kidded her, "Maybe you could loan me a couple thousand." Juanita said, "Yes, me too. I could use some money." Maria said, "You both love the charter fishing business. Each of you probably makes more than I do." They all laughed.

Juanita whispered in Bill's ear, "Can I sleep with you this morning. I promise to let you sleep." Bill said, "Anita might as well come over also. Jeff won't mind, as long as she lets him sleep. We need our sleep so we can catch the big blue marlin." Anita said, "I will let you sleep, Jeff. I promise." The four went to the motel room and took their clothes off. They climbed in bed and went to sleep, with the naked girls cuddling up close to the men they were learning to admire and lust for. Jeff thought, "This is too good to be true." Bill thought, "I love this place. I'm having a great time!" Soon they were all asleep.

Carlos and Maria took all the fish to the fish market. The market had a pier that was a couple hundred yards north of the motel. A man named Juan Martinez helped them unload the fish. He weighed the two flounder for them. Juan was muscular and short with black hair and moustache. His muscles bulged as he wrestled with the large flounder. First he weighed the smallest flounder. It weighed 312 pounds. Next he weighed the biggest fish. He exclaimed, "Que Grande! En todo mi vida, nada tan grande." Carlos said, "You've never seen one so big? How heavy is it?" Juan said, "450 pounds." Carlos said, "It must be a new record. The man who caught it will be a happy man." Juan offered to pay him for the fish. Carlos said, "Butcher all the fish and keep what you want for the work. The rest will go to the poor. We will send them here to get the meat. Be nice to them. They are friends of ours. God smiles on those who help poor people." Juan said, "I will treat them well. I myself am no rich man. No estoy rico." Maria said, "I want you to bring your wife and stay two nights at my motel. Everything is free for you there. Come next week, before we get busy with tourists. It is called El Pesca Grande. We are only a couple hundred yards to the south of you. You know where it is, don't you?" Juan said, "I know where it is. We'll be there this coming weekend. Did you say free food and beer too?" Maria said, "Yes. It is all free to you.

We will bring you more fish for the poor this week. We have two American fishermen staying at the motel, who love to catch many fish." Juan said, "I will give all the fish to the poor. The market won't charge for the processing. We can do our part for the poor, too." He excused himself while he went to talk to his boss. When he returned he had the boss with him. His name was Marco Vargas. He said, "It is admirable that you are helping the poor with so much food. I have decided that I don't want to sell day old fish anymore. Tell the poor people you know, that they can come here at 5:00 o'clock each day. They can have the fish that haven't sold each day." Maria said, "That is generous of

you. I will tell father Romerez. He will spread the word amongst
the poor people that he knows."

Mr. Vargas said, "I would like you to ask the father to issue
letters with his signature to the poor so that I can tell for sure who
is poor. Most people are honest, but I know that some people
with plenty of money might want to get free fish. I don't want to
hurt my daily sales with the free fish program." Maria said, "I
will do as you ask. I'm sure the father will want to help." Carlos
and Maria returned to their boat and motored back to the motel
pier. They tied up the boat and went to the motel for breakfast.
They sat at a table that looked out over the sea. Carlos said, "I
don't know what to think about you owning the motel. Will you
still want a man who has no money?" Maria said, "I could never
find another man like you. If you want me to stop tempting the
tourists, I will. I just think it's good for business. I could hire a
girl to do it for me." Carlos said, "I don't mind if you dance
naked and give back rubs. I do get jealous when you do more
than that." Maria said, "I think we should get secretly married. I
would be loyal to you, but my father would never consent to our
marriage. He would take the motel back." Carlos said, "I don't
want to pit you against your father. It's fun being sneaky out on
the pier with you. If I out live your father, then we can marry. He
is 15 years younger than I am. I won't hold my breath waiting for
him to die. We can just be happy with what we have."

Maria said, "I will put you on the payroll for the motel. I can
pay you for the guests that you take fishing. You can still collect
from them as well. If you save all your money, you will eventually
be wealthy enough that my father will respect you. Limit your
beer drinking so you can take out the morning charter as well as
the afternoon. That will double your income." Carlos said, "What
about Anita and Juanita?" Maria said, "There are enough
customers for all of you. Last year there were fishermen who didn't
go out, because there was no one to take them. I will buy an
additional boat. Then you can all take fishermen out on charters."
Carlos said, "I will limit the beer to three beers. I will count
them, I promise." Maria said, "I would like to marry you, but you

need money to impress my father. I will continue to make love to you even if we don't ever marry. I love the way you make me feel. No one has ever excited me the way you do." She reached across the table and took his hand. It was rough and cracked. She said, "You could try to do something about your hands. If they weren't so rough, I'd let you touch me below the waist." Carlos said, "I'll start using lotion. I'll wear gloves with vasoline inside. That should soften them up." Maria said, "It'll take a month for those hands to soften. I'm eager to let you try. Don't forget. Vasoline in the gloves every day." Carlos said, "I promise. I want you to be perfectly happy. You'll have to show me where to put my fingers. I've never done any of that before." Maria said, "I'll show you. I'm delighted with what you do for me now. I just want us to be more like other people. The man always puts his hands on the woman." Carlos said, "I wouldn't want us to change what we do, but we can add that, too. That will be fine with me." Maria squeezed his hand. "I've never said this to you before, Carlos. She leaned across the table and said softly, "I love you." Carlos said, "You are a good woman. I love you too."

Their breakfast arrived and they ate the bacon, eggs and toast with eagerness. Maria said, "I will convince my father to loan me money to start another motel in my own name. He will love to hear that I long for more money. Once the other motel earns me enough money I can pay my father back. Then I will be independent. He won't be able to stop us from being publicly married." Carlos said, "That will take at least five years. It would be better if we were secretly married now. If I would die, I would like to be married. Then I would not be so likely to go to hell." Maria said, "I know what you mean. I would like to feel that it is acceptable to God for us to be together. It is exciting to be naughty, but we never know when we might die. I don't want to go to hell either." Carlos said, "Will you marry me right away. I know father Romerez. He will marry us secretly." Maria said, "I will marry you, Carlos. I will marry you as soon as the father agrees to do it. You can talk to him today." Carlos said, "I will go talk to him right away. Will you excuse me?" He stood up and pulled her up from her chair. He gave her a big hug and a long French kiss. Maria said, "I will give you a couple thousand dollars for the rings. My money is yours now, and yours is mine. Carlos said, "Yes, we own everything together." He followed her to her room and she gave him the money.

He went to talk to father Romerez first. The father said, "She is very young. Won't her father object?" Carlos said, "Maria thinks he would object. We want to be married secretly by you. I will have more money in 5 or 6 years. Then we will marry publicly." Father Romerez said, "When do you want to be married?" Carlos said, "We have been sinning together for a long time. We want the sin to end. Please marry us soon." Father Romerez said, "I love to put an end to sinning. Both of you come to the church this afternoon. I will marry you." Carlos thanked the father and ran to the jewelry store. He bought a nice one carat diamond for Maria and a band for both of them. He ran back to the motel and found Maria. He said, "The father will marry us at 1:00 o'clock this afternoon. He got on one knee and presented the ring to her. He said, "Will you marry me?" Maria said, "I will." She put on the rings and he put on his. They went to her room and kissed for a long time. Maria said, "I long to do some more things with you, but I don't want to sin right before we go to the church." Carlos said, "I agree. I will go buy a suit so that I am ready for the wedding at 1:00 o'clock." Maria said, "A suit will cause lots of interest and questions. I like you best dressed the way you are. Just put on something clean with no holes." Carlos said, "You're right. We don't want people asking questions." Maria said, "I will only wear my rings when I am with you. You can wear yours all the time. Just say that you like rings." Carlos frowned a little, and then smiled. I guess you're right. If you have on a diamond people will know that something is going on."

They parted company till 12:30 o'clock. Carlos came to the motel and walked Maria to the church. Father Romerez was waiting for them. He performed a nice simple service for them and gave them his blessing. They returned to the motel and sat at their favorite table for lunch. They both ordered lobster. Maria said, "I would like you to continue sleeping on the pier. You know how I love to sneak up on you when you are sleeping." Carlos said, "I don't mind. I love to listen to the sea and smell the water." Maria said, "I want you to keep your clothes in my room. It is now our room, but we need to call it my room. I will do your laundry. After all, I am you wife. Sometimes we can come back to my room and sleep together after we have had sex on the pier." Carlos said, "I like that plan. We can have the best of both worlds. The excitement that we had before, and the closeness of sleeping together like man and wife." Maria said, "I will stay a virgin till we are publicly married. That way I won't anger my father by getting pregnant." Carlos said, "That is fine with me. I am happy with what we are doing now. I don't want you to have trouble with your father. When we are publicly married, I would like lots of children." Maria said, "Don't worry. When the time comes, I will give you many children."

Carlos and Maria spent the afternoon sleeping in her bed. She put her arm around him as she slept. It felt good to have a man with her while she slept. In their sleep they would switch sides, and he would put his arm around her. She felt his rough hands on her side and butt. When he moved his hand to her breasts, she would gently move them away. His fingers were too rough. She wanted his hands on her breasts, but she had to wait till they were softer. They were just too rough. When six o'clock came, Maria's alarm clock went off. She woke up Carlos and they took a shower together.

Down on the main floor Bill had awakened and took Juanita to the shower. They caressed and kissed under the hot steamy water. Finally they came out and dressed for supper. The girls had brought some clothing with them. Jeff woke up and took Anita into the shower. They too caressed and kissed under the hot water. They rubbed soap on each other and scrubbed gently. Finally everyone was clean and dressed. They went to the dining room and drank coffee until Carlos and Maria appeared. When they appeared they sat at the table with the other four. Maria said, "I have a secret to share. You must all promise to keep the secret. If you don't, I could lose the motel and have plenty of trouble with my father. They all promised to keep the secret. Maria said, "Carlos and I were married today at the church." Juanita said, "Congratulations to both of you." The others all said their congratulations. Jeff said, "Tonight's supper on the beach will be a wedding celebration." Maria said, "The cook should have our food about ready. Let's all go to the beach."

They went down by the shore, and saw that the cook was busy at work creating a feast fit for a king. A blanket was set with plates and silverware. They all sat down and waited for the cook to bring the shrimp, lobster and crab meat he had prepared. They all ate the food while the motels entertainer played guitar and sang. The cook put away his cooking supplies and one of the kitchen helpers lit the bonfire. As the sun set, the water took on an orange and red coloring. There was little wind. Maria sent for more blankets. The couples stretched out in each others arms and listened to the small waves that were lapping at the beach. After the guitarist was done, he put on a tape of 1960s hits. The couples listened well into the night and then fell asleep on the beach.

When the sun came up the next morning, they all awoke to the sound of a gentle breeze that was blowing. Carlos said, "I will be a good day to fish for blue marlin. They all went into the motel and ate a big breakfast. Afterwards they drank coffee while Carlos went to buy bait. It didn't take him long. They all went to the pier and got on the panga. Maria had asked one of the kitchen helpers to bring them a large cooler full of ice. The young man came out to the boat with the cooler on a cart. He loaded the cooler onto the boat. Maria said, "Thank you Jaimie. I appreciate your help." He said, "Glad to help, Maria." He turned away and went back to the motel.

Carlos started the engine and everyone sat down. He steered the boat out to sea. Jeff said, "What are we using for bait today?" Carlos said, "Squid. I think it will work well. They had plenty of it, nice and fresh, at the market." Carlos steered straight east for about 30 minutes. Seagulls were everywhere calling out with their characteristic cries. Then Carlos stopped the boat. He said, "Who wants to fish first?" Jeff said, "Bill can go first. I'll try after him." Bill said, "That's fine. I'll give it a try." Juanita and Anita strapped him into the fighting chair while Carlos baited the hook. After Carlos had baited the hook, he put on some gloves. Maria smiled and said, "He's wearing the gloves for me. They will soften his hands." Juanita and Anita whispered to each other and started to giggle. Anita said, "What will he be doing with his hands?" Maria said, "That is up to him. I will only offer suggestions." The two girls giggled some more and then went back to work. They strapped the heavy rod and reel fast to the fighting chair so that it couldn't be jerked overboard. Carlos said, "I will troll the bait fast. If a marlin moves in on the bait, let him have it for a few seconds before you set the hook. Then set it hard. The marlin has a tough jaw. You need to jerk hard several times to make sure the hook is set." Bill said, "I will do just as you say. Let's go."

Carlos started moving the boat at the proper speed for a fast troll. They moved south for about 30 minutes until a marlin started following the boat. It took the bait after a short time. Bill let it have the bait for a few seconds and then jerked hard on the rod. He set the hook well. The marlin felt the sting of the hook and dove deep. The reel sang loudly as line swept overboard and out of sight. Jeff tightened the drag a little for Bill. When the line stopped feeding out so fast, Bill started reeling in. He pumped the rod the way he had seen Jeff do when they fished for muskies in Indiana. When he had gotten back 200 yards of line, the marlin dove deep again. This time it nearly emptied the spool of line. Finally it stopped going down and just held steady. Bill started reeling in line again. Juanita brought him some water and held it to his lips. She said, "Beer would just make you thirsty. This water will be better for you." She tipped up the glass so that he could drink. He kept turning the crank. He said, "Thank you, Juanita." Steadily he kept on lifting the rod and then cranking it back down. The sun was starting to warm things up, and sweat was pouring off Bill's face. He cranked for about an hour until he first saw the marlin. It jumped about 200 yards out. Bill cranked harder than ever and the marlin kept jumping.

Slowly it moved closer to the boat. Jeff found the net and was waiting for the fish at the side of the boat. Bill said, "So, you think I might land this baby. I hope I do, after all this work." He tightened the drag a little more and cranked steadily. The fish was starting to come in a little easier now. It felt heavy. After another 20 minutes the fish was beside the boat. Jeff netted it and the girls helped him pull it aboard. Carlos said, "That marlin weighs about 200 pounds. It's a nice sized fish." Bill said, "Take my picture with it, Jeff." Jeff got the camera and took a picture. Then Bill said, "Get one with Juanita in the picture." Jeff took another picture. Then they released the marlin unharmed.

Next Jeff sat in the chair. The girls strapped him in and fastened the rod and reel to the chair. Carlos baited the hook. Maria watched with interest as he worked. The bait was thrown overboard and Carlos started the boat. They trolled at the usual speed. In about an hour a large blue marlin started following the boat. It took the bait. Jeff let it have the bait for a few seconds and then set the hook. He jerked twice more, to make sure the hook had set. The fish was angered by the pain of the hook jerking into its jaw. It took off, swimming far and deep. Jeff lost nearly all his line right away. He asked Carlos to steer towards the fish so that he could get some line back. Carlos said, "If I do that, you won't have a chance to get into the record books. It is against the official rules. I forgot to tell you. Your flounder was a record setter. It was the biggest they had ever seen at the fish market." Jeff said, "That makes me happy, but today I'm not interested in a record. I just don't want this fish to rip all the line right out of this reel. It is about to do that. I don't want to lose your line." Carlos said, "Sounds good to me." He drove the boat toward the fish while Jeff reeled wildly, trying to get back as much line as he could. Jeff said, "I've got half of the line back." Carlos stopped the boat and waited. Jeff cranked and cranked. He wanted that fish. He was determined not to lose it.

After about two hours the fish surfaced and jumped into the air. Jeff said, "It's a giant!" Bill said, "It sure is. It makes mine look like a baby." Jeff cranked faster on the reel. He was making progress, slow but sure. Anita brought Jeff some water and held the glass up for him to drink. He drank a little, and said, "Thank you, Anita. You are very thoughtful." Anita said, "I will give you some more in a little while. You're working very hard." Jeff said, "This is hard work, but it's fun too. I want a picture of us with this fish." He kept on cranking. Finally the fish came along side the boat. Bill grabbed the net and put the net over the head of the fish. The girls and Carlos helped him try to pull the fish onto the boat. It was too big to lift. Carlos said, "That fish weighs about 1500 pounds. We would have to drag it to the market to weigh it. Shall I release it?" Jeff said, "Yes, go ahead and release it. I'll take a picture of it there in the water." He took a picture and then Carlos released the fish. It swam away slowly. Carlos said, "It will survive. We didn't hurt it too much." Jeff said, "Bill, take a picture of me with Anita, will you?" Bill took the picture. Anita said, "Would you like to get under the blanket with me, Jeff." He said, "That sounds very nice, Anita. First I would like to catch a smaller fish." She kissed him and said, "I will help you catch the fish." She strapped him back into the chair. Carlos baited the hook.

He threw the baited hook overboard. Then he drove the boat at the usual trolling speed for blue marlin. In about an hour Jeff hooked another marlin. This one was of manageable size. He let the fish take out most of the line, and then started pumping and cranking. Jeff fought the fish for 40 minutes before it surfaced. It jumped magnificently. He looked a little tired after another hour went by. His muscles were bulging from cranking so long. Anita brought him some more water to drink. She held it to his lips, and wiped the sweat off his brow. Finally, about 50 minutes later, he brought the fish along side the boat. Bill grabbed the net and netted the fish. The girls helped him bring it onto the deck. Anita unstrapped Jeff from the fighting chair. Jeff said, "Now I can get that picture of me with a blue marlin." Bill got the camera and took a picture of Jeff with the fish. Then Bill said, "Anita, get in the picture. He wants one with you in it." Anita said, "I know. Here I am." She joined Jeff beside the fish. Bill took the picture. Carlos said, "This one is about the same size as the first fish we caught." Jeff said, "Well, Bill, have you had enough marlin fishing. I'd like to go back to the motel and take a cat nap so we can come out fishing for grouper and flounder tonight." Bill said, "That sounds good to me. Carlos is that a good idea?" Carlos said, "I'd be glad to bring all of you back out tonight. The weather is supposed to be nice. The poor people will be glad to get more fish." Carlos steered the boat towards the motel pier. He went slowly, because Jeff and Bill had Juanita and Anita under blankets. He didn't even try to guess what they were doing. Juanita was doing her usual moaning, and Anita was being perfectly quiet. Maria said, "Our guests seem to be enjoying themselves." Carlos said, "Yes, I think they will return in a couple months." In about 45 minutes the boat was coming close to shore. Carlos said, "We are almost home. We'll need some help tying the boat to the dock." The love birds took the hint and came out from under the blankets. They were all sweaty and breathing hard. Maria said, "You will all need showers." Juanita said, "We like showers. It won't be a problem."

The boat pulled up along side the pier. Juanita and Anita jumped out and tied the boat fast. They all went to the motel and showered in pairs. They spent a long time in the water. Jeff and Anita had to wait for Bill and Juanita to get finished. When they were done, Jeff and Anita eagerly went to the shower. Anita said, "How much longer can you stay?" Jeff said, "We have to leave on Saturday. I don't want my wife to be suspicious. We said we would only be gone about a week." Anita asked, "When will you return?" Jeff said, "This is Thursday the 17th. We will come back on the 15th of July. We can't do any petting on Saturday. Bill and I need to be horny when we return to our wives, or they will be suspicious." Anita said, "I understand. Juanita and I will say goodbye on Friday. I don't want our last day together to be without petting. We will go stay with our parents for a day." Jeff said,

"That will be fine. Bill and I will fish for red snapper that day. They won't tire us out before our long drive home." Jeff and Anita finished drying themselves and then crawled in bed for a nap. They slept naked as usual. They slept with their arms around each other.

At 8:00 o'clock in the evening Maria's alarm clock went off. She woke up and got dressed in her bikini. She woke up Carlos and he got dressed too. They went down to the main floor and woke up Jeff, Bill and the girls. They all got dressed and went to the dining room for a late supper. They had wet burritos and homemade bread with butter. They took their time and drank plenty of strong coffee. They all drank instant Folgers. The guests preferred it to brewed coffee.

When they were finished, they went to the boat. The cooler full of ice and beer had already been placed on the boat. Carlos said, "We can use the left over squid from today for the bait. They are here in the cooler with the beer." Anita and Juanita untied the boat and Carlos steered them out to their favorite fishing spot. When they reached the fishing spot, Carlos shut off the motor and Juanita and Anita baited the hooks. They threw the baited hooks into the water. In no time at all, Jeff and Bill were catching grouper. The fish averaged around 50 pounds each. They released the smaller ones. Jeff said, "We want to fish legal. Only 10 fish for each of us." Carlos said, "Yes, I don't want to pay a fine, or lose my license." Maria said, "The conservation agents can even take the boat if they want to. It belongs to the motel. I don't want to lose it. They cost around $20,000. Soon I will be buying another boat, so that Juanita and Anita can take out one group in the morning and Carlos can take a different group at the same time." Carlos said, "I will keep this boat. I am used to it. The girls can have the new boat."

Juanita said, "I like new boats. I don't mind taking the new boat." Anita said, "Yes, a new boat will be fine." In an hour Jeff and Bill each had nine grouper. Now they were fishing for flounder. They each wanted to catch one flounder to fill out their quota of fish. Jeff was the first to hook one. It took a lot of effort, but he managed to bring it up to the side of the boat. Carlos gaffed it and the girls helped him bring it into the boat. Carlos said, "This one weighs about 200 pounds." He sat back down at the steering wheel and waited for Bill to catch his fish. It was an hour till Bill hooked one. He reeled it in ruthlessly. He wanted this fish badly. He knew that when he had it on the boat, he could have some time with Juanita. He cranked hard on the reel, pumping the rod like a professional. Finally the fish came to the surface. It was bigger than the one Jeff had caught. Carlos gaffed the fish, and everyone helped him bring it onto the deck. Carlos said, "This one must weigh 350 pounds." They dragged the fish to the front of the boat where they would be out of the way. The girls brought Jeff and Bill each a beer. They drank several more as Carlos steered the boat home.

Friday morning the wind picked up and fishing was out of the question. Carlos arrived at Jeff and Bill's door to tell them the bad news. He handed Bill a handful of viagra and said, "I'm sure you can find something to do in the room with the girls." Bill smiled and took the viagra. He woke Jeff and the girls. They got dressed and went to the dining room for breakfast. They all ate a big breakfast. Jeff and Bill had viagra with their orange juice. The girls saw them take the pills and started giggling. They all ate their breakfast and had some coffee. Then they all hurried to the room. Maria knocked on the door and Jeff opened it. Maria said, "Jeff, you can take Anita to my room for the day. I'm sure you would like some privacy." Jeff said, "Thanks. It would be nice." He and Anita followed Maria to her room. The two couples spent the day with the two virgins doing what they knew how to do so well. Jeff and Bill had a day that they would never forget.

When they were finally sated, Anita said, "You must return sooner if you can. It will be hard to wait three months for you to come back." Jeff said, "We may come back in a month. We just need to come up with a reason that will satisfy our wives. I thought we might start our own charter business down here. Then we could come down every month to check on things." Anita said, "That's a good idea. There are plenty of tourists who want to fish.

You wouldn't have to make a lot of money. Just so you didn't lose money." Jeff said, "Exactly! I'll run this by Bill. He doesn't have much money, but both of us have good credit. We could borrow the money for a boat and small motel." Anita said, "You could buy part interest in the motel that Maria is going to start up this year. I'm sure she would like to have help." Jeff said, "I'll talk to her about it."

Anita helped Jeff pack his suitcase and then she went with him to meet the others for breakfast. They had the usual bacon and eggs with toast. They all drank Folgers coffee. Jeff said to Maria, "Bill and I need an excuse to come here every month. Would you let us be partners in you new motel?" Maria said, "I would like to, but I am afraid that one of you might divorce his wife. Then she would want to sell and I would be in a bind." Jeff said, "I never thought of that. You are right to have those reservations." Maria said, "I will hire you both as part time maintenance men. You could come for two weeks out of every month and get my motels in excellent shape before you leave again. I could pay you enough to cover your monthly expenses. You won't get rich at it." Jeff said, "I like that idea. What about you, Bill?" Bill said, "I think it would be great. My wife has been wishing that I would get a job, and I can't stand the factories." Jeff said, "I just hope that my wife likes the idea. She may not want me gone that much. Maybe if I just stayed one week every month." Maria said, "What ever hours you want to work will be fine with me. It is up to you." Jeff said, "Fine then. I think my wife will go along with that."

Jeff said, "Until the motel is built, I think Anita and Juanita should go on some fishing trips with Bill and me. I will call the motel here to say when we will come to pick them up. I think I'd like us to go to Alaska next month." Bill said, "That sounds good to me." Juanita said, "I'll go with you." Anita said, "Yes, we should have plenty of money from the tourists by then. I'd love to see Alaska."

They finished their meal and then Anita and Juanita went to stay with their parents. Jeff helped Bill finish packing. Jeff said,

"I would leave my wife for a girl like Anita, but what if she would start to take me for granted too. It seems that after you marry a woman, the sex goes down hill." Bill said, "I think you're right. These girls will eventually want lots of children. I don't think I'm up for that. We can enjoy them for a few years. Then we may have to move on to some younger girls. These girls are a rare find, but I think we could do it again if we had too." Jeff said, "I'm getting quite attached to Anita. I hope we can keep this going for a long time." Bill said, "I agree. I'm going to try to make it go on for as long as possible. We are lucky guys. You don't find many girls like Anita and Juanita. Young women usually go after older guys for money. I think that these girls are after good sex and companionship." Jeff said, "You're right. They are a couple wonderful girls. We should keep them as long as we can."

The two men found Carlos and paid him for the fishing charter trips. They also gave him some money to give the girls later, for their charter work. Carlos took them out one last time on the boat. They toured along the coast and looked at the houses. After a couple hours, they fished for red snapper and caught 20 nice ones. Carlos steered them slowly back to the pier. Jeff said, "Why don't we go with you to the fish market?" Carlos said, "That'll be fine." In a short time they were at the fish market and dropped off the fish. Jeff and Bill looked around the market for awhile and then had Carlos take them back to the motel.

They ate lunch with Carlos and Maria. Maria told them where the new motel would be. She said, "I asked my father for the financing this morning. He was delighted and was happy to hear that I had already arranged for part time maintenance men to work at the new motel. He is going to have the construction start next month. He is also financing me for two more boats. I will have fishing charters at each motel." Bill said, "You are lucky to have a father that is generous." Maria said, "He wants me to make money like he does. It makes him proud. I have finally learned how to get along with him."

After lunch the men said goodbye to Carlos and Maria. They put their suit cases in the Saturn and headed for home. They took turns driving as fast as they thought they could get away with. The deserted Mexican highways were great for high speed driving. In 30 hours they were pulling into the drive at Jeff's place. It was 7:00 o'clock in the evening on Monday. They each took their suit cases into the house and greeted their wives. Nancy was glad to see Jeff. She said, "How many fish did you catch?" Jeff said, "We caught a couple hundred. The fish were biting very well." Nancy said, "I got your post cards, did you miss me?" Jeff said, "Yes. Of course I missed you." Nancy said, "I'll put some pizza in the oven. You can watch television or read a book." Jeff said, "Thanks, I think I will."

Over at Bill's, things were going well. He had his wife on the floor in front of the stove. They were making love. Sandy said, "Well, I can see that you missed me." She stroked his hair as he let her have the big one. He was thinking how glad he was that he had not had sex on Saturday. He appreciated Sandy's nice slender body. He liked her blonde hair and blue eyes. He knew, however, that she didn't crave him every day like Juanita did. Her sex drive was starting to wane. She usually only wanted him on Sunday. Once a week was plenty for her. She accused him of struggling to stay young. How he wished there was a viagra for women. He knew Sandy would always be here for him. Juanita was so young that she could change as she got older. Possibly Juanita would not always find him so attractive. He wanted to keep both women. He would have to try his best to keep his secret from Sandy.

Nancy brought the pizza to Jeff and sat with him to watch television. Jeff watched her and admired her slender body. She looked great for her age. She always kept her brown hair looking nice. He had always liked her large breasts. They ate the pizza and discussed the fishing trip. Jeff said, "I caught a very large blue marlin, but we couldn't get it onto the boat. We released it. Bill caught a smaller one. We released all the marlin." Nancy said, "Why did you let them go?" Jeff said, "The charter captain said it would be best to let them go so that other people could catch them. If the supply would ever be threatened, it would hurt the tourist industry." Nancy said, "That sounds like good planning." Jeff said, "We gave lots of fish to the poor people of Loreto." Nancy said, "That is noble. Where do you plan on fishing next?" Jeff said, "We talked about going to Alaska. There are big salmon and trout there. The guided trips there are expensive, but if we find a good spot on our own, it won't cost much." Nancy said, "Just the gasoline will cost several hundred dollars. I don't think you can afford a trip every couple weeks." Jeff said, "Bill and I have a plan to get more money for fishing trips. While we were at Loreto we got to know the owner of the motel we were staying at. He said he is opening another motel in a month from now, and will need some maintenance people. Bill and I offered to work for two weeks out of every month. We can fish there during the time we work and then be home for two weeks each month. We'd just do it until we grow tired of the area, but the fishing there is sensational." Nancy said, "If that's what you want to do. I know you will come back to me. Even fishing in Mexico will lose its charm after awhile." Jeff said, "I'm glad you consent. I probably will grow tired of it after awhile. Bill and I want to go to Alaska next Monday. Is that O.K. with you?" Nancy said, "As long as you have enough money. Just call me every night. You didn't call on this last trip." Jeff said, "I'll call plenty. I just didn't know how to use the phones down there. I thought they would be real expensive." Jeff asked his wife to go upstairs with him and she consented. They did the same thing they always did. Jeff didn't complain about the monotony. He was just glad that his wife was going along with his new plans. He thought that he had better beg for a blow job like he always did. He didn't want her to think something was wrong. As he expected, she refused. They both managed to have an orgasm and then went to sleep.

At Bill's house he brought up the new fishing plan, "Sandy, I promised Jeff that I'd fish with him in Alaska on May 1st. Since all these fishing trips cost money, he and I agreed to do maintenance work at the motel in Loreto. We want to start in a month from now when a new motel opens up. We would work two weeks and then be off two weeks. We can fish down there during the two weeks that we are working. Then we can be home for two weeks. We'd only do this until we get tired of fishing there. Maybe a couple years." Sandy said, "I'm glad to see that you are becoming industrious. I was afraid you would become bored and depressed in your later years. If this will make you happy, and we can afford it, go ahead and have fun. Nancy and I can keep each other company here while you are gone. You must call every night though. You didn't call once on this trip." Bill said, "With a job, I'll be able to afford the phone bill." Bill said, "Jeff and I want to leave next Monday for the Alaska trip. Is that acceptable?" Sandy said, "Sure. Just remember to call every night." Bill said, "I will. I promise." They took a hot shower together and put on there robes. They watched television till bed time. Sandy said, "You sent some nice post cards from Loreto. That was very thoughtful of you." Bill said, "I knew you'd like to here from me. They have beautiful beaches down there with palm trees everywhere." Sandy said, "You must take me with you sometime next year. I'll have some vacation days accumulated by then." Bill said, "That'll be great. I think you would enjoy Loreto." They chatted more about possible vacations and then fell asleep.

In the morning Jeff called Bill on the phone. He said, "Let's go bluegill fishing on Syracuse Lake." Bill said, "I'm not doing anything else. I'll go. When do you want to leave?" Jeff said, "Let's go right now." Bill said, "We can eat breakfast over there at the restaurant." Jeff said, "I'll pick you up in 10 minutes. I'm going to have a cup of coffee first." Bill said, "I'll be ready." They hung up the phones and Jeff got his coffee.

Jeff drove up to Bill's house and honked the horn. Bill came out and they drove to Syracuse pulling Jeff's new boat. They stopped at the restaurant and had breakfast. Jeff said, "My wife said she doesn't mind if we go to Alaska on May 1st. She also said I can work in the Loreto motel." Bill said, "My wife went along with everything too. She wants to see Loreto next year. Do you think that would get us into trouble?" Jeff said, "I think we could count on the girls to stay out of the way. I know Maria would cover for us. I said that a man owned the motel. We'll have to ask Maria to have Carlos play the owner while your wife is down there. I think we could pull it off. I thought my wife might get suspicious if I said that we'd be working for a woman. I was probably just being too careful." Bill said, "Yes, the truth might have been better. Maybe I'll say there are lots of snakes in Loreto. Sandy hates snakes. Maybe she will settle for a trip to Florida."

They finished the breakfast and went to the boat launch on the south end of the lake. Jeff launched the boat with Bill in it. Bill used the trolling motor to guide the boat back to the pier. Jeff got in the boat and they went to one of Jeff's favorite fishing spots. They started catching bluegill right away. It was a little early for bluegill, but the recent warm weather was helping matters. Jeff said, "I miss the girls already." Bill said, "So do I. I wish I had two lives to live. One with my wife, and one with Juanita." Jeff said, "Yes, I felt a little guilty when my wife was so happy to see me back, but she just doesn't care about my sexual needs. She doesn't understand how important sex is to me. I need some variety." Bill said, "I know what you mean. My wife isn't as bad as yours about that. I just got tempted by the stunning beauty of Juanita. And she is so young. It's flattering as hell to have a young beauty like that throwing herself at you."

Jeff said, "I wonder if they are like that with lots of other tourists. I don't really mind if they do. I just wonder about it." Bill said, "Me too. I wonder if they are actually in love with us, or just doing what they are in the habit of doing. They could make lots of money that way. We didn't tip them much at all. They didn't seem to want that from us." Jeff said, "Yeah, I didn't think they wanted our money. Something just made them respond to us. I'll go to a pay phone and call Loreto today to tell the girls that we'll pick them up April 28th. Bill said, "That sounds like a good idea. Where will we stay in Alaska?" Jeff said, "I have a large canvas cabin tent with a stove. We can camp with them at Katmai National Park and Preserve. It's part of the Aleutian Range. It will be cold up there. I'll buy a pair of sleeping bags for two. The fishing there is supposed to be excellent. We can find a charter somewhere near there to take us out for halibut fishing.

Halibut get pretty big there. We can take the Alaskan Highway to Anchorage. The Aleutian Range is just south of there.

Bill said, "It sounds like you have this pretty well planned. I hope the girls will like the cold weather. We might need to buy them some warm clothes." Jeff said, "I was planning on us keeping them in the sleeping bags most of the time." Bill said, "That sounds good." Jeff said, "Seriously though, they said they would have plenty of money. They can buy some warm coats. That's about all they'll need. My tent gets nice and warm with a wood fire in the stove. They'll need warm coats to go out in the boat we charter."

They caught 30 bluegill in all. It was 3:00 o'clock in the afternoon when they returned to the boat launch and pulled the boat out. They went home and cleaned the fish. Jeff said, "Why don't you and Sandy come over for fried fish tonight?" Bill said, "That sounds good. I'll tell Sandy." He went home and told Sandy about the plan. She said, "I'd love to go over and have supper with them." The time passed quickly. In no time at all, Jeff and Bill were on their way to Alaska with a detour to Loreto, Mexico.

As usual they drove at close to 100 m.p.h. They couldn't wait to see the girls again. On Wednesday morning they pulled up to El Pesca Grande. The girls were waiting in the restaurant. When they saw the men, they jumped up and ran to them. They hugged them eagerly. Juanita said, "You should stay here today and rest. You have already driven a long way. It is even further to Alaska." Jeff said, "You talked me into it. What shall we do first?" Anita said, "We reserved a free room for each of you. Come with me Jeff. I will show you your room. Juanita has one for Bill." They went to the rooms. The men were tired but they hugged and kissed the girls for a long time. Then they fell asleep for five or six hours. While they slept the girls had fun playing with their bodies. They were careful not to wake the men, but they made sure their dreams were full of fun.

The girls finally left the men and went to the restaurant for coffee. Juanita said, "What did you and Jeff do?" Anita said, "I think he is dreaming of sex now. I gave him what he needs to sleep soundly. It sure was easy. He must have really needed what I gave him. We may need to drive for the first day. I think he will be a little tired." Juanita said, "They aren't that old. I did the same thing with Bill, but I'm sure he'll be able to drive. We should leave at midnight. There is less traffic at night." Anita said, "The men will decide when they wake up."

At 5:00 o'clock in the afternoon the men got up and went to the dining room. Maria and Carlos were sitting with Juanita and Anita drinking coffee. Maria said, "Welcome. Come and join us. I haven't seen you two for awhile." Jeff said, "It's good to be back." They sat and ordered some coffee. Bill said, "My wife wants to come down here next year. Jeff told his wife that we would be employed by a man so that his wife wouldn't get jealous. Can we say that Carlos owns the motels?" Maria said, "That'll be fine. He's my partner now. We own them together. That is, we will own them when the other one is built." Bill said, "That takes a load off my mind. I was afraid there might be some complications." Jeff said, "I knew everything would work out fine." Carlos said, "When will you leave for Alaska? Won't it be quite cold up there this time of year?" Jeff said, "I think we should leave late this evening. The traffic won't be bad then. You're right. The weather on the ocean will be cold. We brought heavy coats. The girls can buy some when we get to Washington. There will be stores there that have left over winter coats for sale." Juanita said, "We each have quite a bit of money. How much should we each bring?" Jeff said, "Three thousand should be more than enough. You will each only need about $500, but it's good to have plenty of cash when you're that far from home. I have a credit card for myself." Juanita said, "I'll bring three thousand. We might want to stay in some nice motels along the way." Anita said, "I agree. Some nice motels would be nice. Hot tubs and swimming pools would be a nice relaxation after long days of driving."

Jeff said, "I want us to take a halibut fishing charter. I called the charter service and found out that the one day fee is $500 for five hours. That should be long enough to enjoy a different kind of fishing. I made a reservation for fishing and for a camp site."

Anita said, "That is expensive. I wish we could get that kind of money here." Jeff said, "Everything is expensive in Alaska. It costs them a lot of money to ship things in to them. Everything is remote. Supplies are brought in by plane." Juanita said, "That explains the high prices. Our boat gas is inexpensive, and the food isn't high priced either."

They ate supper together and then took a nice long boat ride. They watched the sun set from the boat. There was little wind. They spent a little while feeding the seagulls. Finally after the sunset they returned to the pier. The moon was bright and they had no trouble seeing to tie up the boat. The girls loaded their suitcases into the Saturn and they all got in the car. Maria and Carlos waved good bye as they drove away.

CHAPTER FOUR

The Alaskan Experience

They left Loreto and headed north. Jeff drove at his usual high speed. They took turns driving, and drove twenty-four hours before they stopped at a motel in Seattle. Jeff found a room with double king size beds. They showered as couples and then went right to bed. They slept naked as usual. They played with each other for awhile. Then Juanita said to Bill, "You said, last time we were together, that I really like to pet. What does that mean?" Bill said, "Petting is when you kiss me and use your mouth on intimate areas. Or it is when I have my hand or mouth on your intimate parts?" Juanita said, "I understand now. You are right, I do like it. Can I do it some more, now? Bill said, "Pet away, honey. Then I'll pet you." They went on for about an hour and then decided to sleep. They had lots of driving to do the next day.

They got up early and continued to follow highway 5 north into Canada. They occasionally saw a black bear near the roadside. About 500 miles north of the border, they saw a moose crossing the road. Juanita said, "I've never seen that animal before. What's it called?" Bill said, "That's a moose. They live in northern Michigan too." Anita said, "I'm glad we don't have them in Mexico. They look dangerous." Jeff said, "They can be dangerous. It's best to stay out of their way. They can swim well. I had one chase me once when I was paddling a canoe on Georgian Bay in Ontario." Bill said, "You never told me that. You've been to lots of places." Jeff said, "Yes, I love to travel. Nature is a big part of what makes a trip interesting. We will probably see some grizzly bears on this trip. They are more dangerous than black bears. We'll stay a long way away from them if we can."

Anita said, "That sounds like a good plan. I don't think I like grizzly bears. Where will we stay in Alaska?" Jeff said, "I brought a big tent, stove and two double sleeping bags. They will be very romantic, and they are warm." Anita said, "I've never slept in a tent. How do you put them up?" Jeff said, "I can do it in 20 minutes. I'll show you when we get there. There are ropes and stakes that hold the tent in place. It is held up by a system of aluminum poles." Juanita said, "That tent will save us money on motels." Jeff said, "Where we're going, there are no motels. We can rent a cabin if we want to. Everything is primitive. We will stay at campgrounds where there are toilets and showers. Unfortunately the men and women have to shower separately." Juanita said, "That will cramp our style a little, but the sleeping bags will make up for it. Can one person be down inside the sleeping bag? Bill said, "I'll leave the zipper down on the side of the bag. I'm looking forward to this camping." Then he laughed.

They drove on for many hours until they came to a small trading post that had a little restaurant with it. They all went inside and ordered late breakfasts. They had ham and eggs with coffee. They bought a cooler and ice. Ham and egg sandwiches were stuffed inside with a gallon of milk. Jeff bought a compass. They also bought some canteens and filled them with water. They bought several six packs of soda pop. They loaded everything in the car and started out again. They drove rapidly and managed to make it to Anchorage in 16 more hours. When they got into town Jeff found a nice motel and they stayed the night. They really appreciated the showers together. They knew that would end soon. After a good night of sleep, they went to a restaurant and had breakfast. They had omelets and coffee. Jeff said, "I'll find a bush plane service in the phone book. We should be able to set up our tent today in the Katmai National Park and Preserve."

Jeff left the table and looked at the phone book. He picked out a plane charter service and called them. They said they would send someone over to the restaurant to guide them to the plane. Jeff went back to the table and told the others. They were all excited. Bill said, "That was easy." Jeff said, "They want to make things easy for tourists so they will come back often." Juanita said, "Will we all fit in one plane?" Jeff said, "That's a good question. They said with the tent we would need two plane rides. They are $200 each round trip. That's not too high." Anita said, "Yes, we can afford that. I'm tired of riding in a car. It will be fun to fly." Juanita said, "I've never been in a plane before. I'm looking forward to it."

In about 30 minutes the charter service representative arrived and led them to the air strip. They were fueling the planes when they arrived. The staff of the charter service quickly loaded the tent and the suitcases onto the planes. In no time they were flying towards the Katmai Park. Jeff and Anita were on the first plane to leave. Jeff said, "You'll like our campsite. It's on a beach that is right on the Pacific Ocean." Anita said, "I'm looking forward to the tent. It sounds cozy. We can have lots of fun in it. We'll be able to hear the waves all night, just like in Loreto." Jeff said, "I'm looking forward to the tent, too. The stove will keep us warm, and I brought along a surprise for everyone." Anita said, "What is it?" Jeff said, "I'll tell you tonight. I don't want to spoil it by telling now." Anita said, "I'll wait, then." She watched out the window as they flew south in the small pontoon plane. She rubbed Jeff's leg gently as the time passed. He put his arm around her and kissed her frequently.

In the other plane Juanita was asking Bill about the park. "What is the park like?" she asked. Bill said, "Jeff told me it is right on the Pacific Ocean. There should be lots of trees and wildlife." Juanita kissed him and said, "This is the most exciting thing I've ever done. Will there be bears?" Bill said, "I'm sure there will be bears. Jeff said we need to hang our food up in trees so the bears can't reach it. He said we should never keep food in the tent or the bears will come right in after the food." Juanita said, "I'm glad Jeff knows about bears. I don't know a single thing about them." She kissed Bill long and hard. She rubbed between his legs as she kissed him. He could feel himself getting excited. Finally she stopped and giggled. "I just can't wait to get into the tent with a fire in the stove. It sounds wonderful and romantic." Bill said, "It will be fun, I am sure. We can stay several days if we want to. We didn't say exactly when we would return. I'd like to stay several weeks." Juanita said, "That sounds good to me."

In a little less than an hour, the planes touched down on the ocean just next to the beach on the Katmai Park. The pilots powered the planes next to the pier. The charter boat guide was waiting for them. He said, "Your fishing charter isn't till tomorrow, but I wanted to meet you all. You're the first fishermen this season. It's still a little too cold for most people." They all introduced themselves. The pilots unloaded the planes and then took off. Their charter captain was named Bill Phillips. He said, "I would like us to leave tomorrow morning at 6:00 o'clock if that is fine with all of you." Juanita said, "We like getting an early start." Bill helped them carry their supplies to the campsite which was only a couple hundred feet away. He said, "Fire wood is included in the campsite fee of $10 per night. My little trading post has a good supply of food if you need it. I try to price things reasonably." Jeff said, "Thanks. We didn't bring much food. We were in a hurry. Anita, why don't you and Juanita go to the store and get some food while Bill and I put up the tent?" Anita said, "I want to see how the tent is put up. Then we'll get the food." Bill said, "I'll have the store open till 5:00 o'clock. It is 3:00 o'clock now. I'll see you folks in the morning. That's my boat there tied to the other side of the pier." Jeff said, "We'll be there on time. I brought my wind up alarm clock."

Jeff and Bill put up the tent while the girls watched them work. They had it up in 20 minutes. They installed the stove and stove pipe. Then they carried plenty of wood for the stove. They put the wood inside the tent so they wouldn't have to go out in the cold for it at night. They also stacked some wood outside for a campfire by the shore. It wasn't windy, but they knew it would be cool in the evening. They would need the fire to keep warm. It was about 50 degrees out. The girls were glad they had bought warm coats in Seattle.

Now that the tent was up, they all went to the trading post to get food. Jeff saw some topographical maps. He bought a couple just because he liked looking at them. The girls each had a basket which they filled with milk, coffee, cereal, eggs and bacon. They bought a skillet and a coffee pot with cups. They also bought paper bowls and plates. Jeff picked out some plastic forks, knives and spoons. Bill found a pancake turner and some pancake mix. They looked the place over carefully. They found salt and pepper for the eggs. Jeff bought a white gas lantern and some white gas. He said, "This will help us see what we are doing. Flashlights tend to go dead. This will be cheaper in the long run. I can take it with us when we leave." The girls insisted on paying for everything. They said, "You can both share the price of the charter with us, but we want to provide the food." Bill said, "I guess it will be fine." Jeff said, "Just don't try to pay for everything." Juanita said, "You paid for the planes. That was $400. Let us pay our share of that." Jeff said, "I'll cover it this time. If we go on another charter we can split the plane fare."

They went to the tent and started the fire in the stove. In about 30 minutes it was ready to cook on. They had pancakes and syrup with coffee and eggs. Jeff started the fire down by the beach while the girls prepared the sleeping bags. Bill had to show them that the self inflating air mats went under the sleeping bags. They were fascinated with how the air mats filled up on their own. Juanita said, "These must have cost a fortune." Bill said, "I think each one is about $130." Juanita said, "This state of the art camping stuff is expensive. How much were the sleeping bags? Did Jeff buy them just for our trip?" Bill said, "Jeff said he paid $300 for each bag. They are expensive since they are goose down." Jeff came into the tent and said, "I got the fire going." Anita said, "You should let us pay for the sleeping bags, Jeff." He said, "If it makes you happy you can pay for half." Anita handed him three hundred dollar bills. She said, "Now I feel better about this. We work full time. You only work one or two weeks per month." Jeff said, "What ever you two want to pay is fine with me. Just don't try to pay for everything. I want you to be eager for the next trip. I don't want you to dread the expense." Anita said, "Don't worry, we have plenty of money."

Anita said, "What was that surprise you had for us?" Jeff said, "After the campfire I'll tell you." Juanita said, "What surprise?" Anita said, "Jeff told me on the plane that he has a surprise for us. I can't wait to know what it is." Jeff said, "Let's go down to the shore and enjoy the fire." They all went to the campfire. Jeff told stories about his fishing and camping trips. Bill sang a couple folk songs that he knew. The girls wanted to go for a swim, but Jeff talked them out of it. He said, "The water is only about 40 degrees. You could easily get sick. It would ruin the whole trip." Juanita said, "You're right. I didn't think the water would be that cold." She ran to the edge of the water and dipped her hand in. "Brrrrrr," she said. "That is extremely cold." Anita ran to the water and dipped her hand in. She said, "I think I can resist swimming. This isn't Mexico. That's for sure."

They sat on some logs and watched the fire as darkness set in. Jeff said, "We need to get up early. I think we should go to the tent and get ready for bed." They all agreed and went to the tent. Jeff lit the white gas lantern. He pumped it up and it shown brightly. He hung it with a coat hanger from the tent roof. Anita said, "Now tell us about the surprise." Jeff said, "O.K." He went over to his duffle bag and pulled out a one gallon jug of body lotion. He said, "I thought it might be fun for you girls to get slippery all over and let us rub you with our bodies." The girls looked at each other and grinned. Juanita said, "You are a clever man, Jeff. Let's do it right away. I can't wait."

The girls opened the sleeping bags and Jeff turned the light off. Only the light from the open stove door revealed the beauty of the girls as they took off their clothes. The men watched them spread the lotion all over their bodies. At the same time they took off all their clothes. The couples crawled into the sleeping bags and the fun began. The girls moaned with delight. They had never felt men in such a way before. They positioned themselves in every way they could think of to give the men the most pleasure. They were so turned on that they were tempted to give the men permission to take them all the way. They wanted it, and they were starting to be terribly tempted. After about an hour the girl's heads disappeared down into the sleeping bags. The men moaned softly as the girls ended the fun for the night by giving the men what they needed. They liked it down deep in the warm sleeping bags. They stayed there a long time. They wanted to be sure that the men were completely satisfied.

The alarm clock went off at 5:00 o'clock. The men watched with pleasure as the slender slippery women walked around before them. They prepared breakfast in the nude. Juanita said, "I was so turned on last night that I wanted to go all the way, Bill. I would like to have a child for you. You need someone to carry on your lineage, someone to bear your name." Bill said, "Who would care for the child?" Juanita said, "I would care for the child and raise him or her. We could tell people in Loreto that we got married in Las Vegas." Bill said, "I like your plan. I do need an heir. Even though all I have to leave someone is my $80,000 house. If I would die before my wife, she would inherit the house. How could I pass it on to our child?" Juanita said, "Don't worry about the money. I have enough money. I want to give you children. You have made me crave you completely. I want to give myself to you like a wife does." Bill said, "It's fine then, whatever you want. I thought you didn't want to ruin your figure." Juanita said, "It will return. I won't eat too much when I'm pregnant. I will stay in shape." Anita said, "I too felt a new longing last night, Jeff. "I want you to take me all the way. I want to have your child." Jeff said, "I'm flattered. Will you care for him or her on your own? I'm not a rich man. I can't take money from my wife and give it to you." Anita said, "Juanita and I are becoming rich from the tourist business, but since we now have a bad reputation in Loreto, no respectable man will marry us. I long to have you like a wife would have you. Please say you will." Jeff said, "Will you get fat and stay fat after you have our child?" Anita said, "I promise to stay in shape. I don't want to lose you." Jeff said, "I will give you what you want then. We can use the lotion again tomorrow night, only I will treat you like a wife." Anita said, "Thank you, Jeff. Thank you."

Juanita said, "We can do the same thing, Bill. I will give you a beautiful child." Bill said, "I want that very much. We can do it tonight, after our fishing trip." They ate a breakfast of eggs and bacon with milk. The girls got dressed and they went out to the pier. Captain Bill was waiting in the boat. He had a golden Labrador retriever with him. He said, "You made it on time. That's good. We can leave right away." He started the engine and they headed south along the coast for about 30 minutes. Then he turned out to the east. After another 20 minutes he cut the engine. He said, "I'll get the rods and reels out. Can you bait your own hooks?" Juanita said, "We can do the baiting. Just show us where the bait is." Bill pointed to a bucket at the stern of the boat. It was half full of herring. He brought out the rods and passed them out. He said, "I'll be happy to do the baiting if you don't want to." Juanita said, "We run a fishing charter in Mexico. It's no problem for us." Bill said, "Well, I'm impressed. There aren't too many women who run fishing charters." They all baited their hooks and threw them overboard. They waited for about 30 minutes until Anita got a bite. It was a heavy fish. She pulled up hard on the rod. Bill said, "You can pry on the side of the boat if you want to. You can't hurt these rods. They are thick and tough." Juanita pried on the side of the boat with all her might. She cranked the reel as hard as she could. After about 25 minutes a halibut surfaced and Captain Bill netted it. He said, "This one weighs about 120 pounds. They reach up to 700 pounds here. This one will make good eating. My customers usually donate the meat to nursing homes on the mainland. Will that be O.K.?" Juanita said, "That will be fine. In Mexico we give the meat to the poor people, too."

Next Jeff got a bite. His fish took an hour to bring in. It weighed 500 pounds. It took everyone's help to get it into the boat. Next,

Anita and Bill got bites. Captain Bill had to get out another net so that Jeff could net one while he netted the other halibut. Both fish weighed around 250 pounds. By the end of the five hours, they had a total of 12 halibut that averaged around 300 pounds each. Captain Bill said, "You are all fine fishermen. I can tell you are experienced. I will cut off enough meat from one of the fish so that you can cook some for supper tonight." Juanita said, "That'll be great!"

Captain Bill steered the boat home while the couples kissed in the back of the boat and watched the scenery. When they returned it was 12:00 o'clock. They went to the tent and built up the fire in the stove. Anita said, "I can't wait till tonight. Let's get out the body lotion and get in the sleeping bags. Jeff said, "That sounds good to me." Jeff and Bill watched as the girls lubed themselves all over. Then they crawled into the sleeping bags with them. They had some wonderful petting and foreplay, but this time they gave the girls what they had been longing for. They bent the girls around like pretzels and had them in many delightful positions. When they were finished, they all got dressed and went for a walk along the shoreline. They walked hand in hand. Anita said, "Wouldn't it be nice if we could be married?" Jeff said, "I think it would be nice, but I could never divorce my wife. She hasn't done anything to deserve that." Anita said, "She always refuses to give you bl-w jobs. Isn't that grounds for divorce?" Jeff said, "I don't know if it is or not. I just don't want to divorce her. I am learning to love you, Anita, but I can't bring myself to contemplate divorcing my wife." Anita said, "Well, at least we can be together often. It will be as though we are married. I will tell people in Loreto that we are married. That way they will respect my child." Jeff said, "That will be fine. We will try to convince Bill's wife not to go to Loreto. I don't know how, but we'll find a way."

Juanita said, "Is it fine with you if I tell people in Loreto that we're married?" Bill said, "That will be fine. I can get my wife to not visit Loreto. I will take her to Florida instead. She has been wanting to go to Florida." Juanita said, "I feel like I am married to you. This is a wonderful fishing trip." They walked for miles and only returned to the tent as the sun was setting. Jeff rekindled the fire in the stove and soon the girls were cooking up some of the halibut on the stove. It smelled good. They cooked with butter and they ate the fish on buttered bread. The halibut was a wonderful fish. It tasted great. When they were done eating, they burned the paper plates in the stove. Juanita said, "This sure beats washing dishes." Bill said, "Yes, this is the way to live. On the way back south, we can stop at some of the campsites south of Fairbanks. I noticed them on the way here." Juanita said, "That will be great, I love camping. The fires look so nice and the sleeping bags are warm." Anita said, "I like camping too. We'll have to go often." Jeff said, "We can even do some camping in Mexico. Only there, we will need to watch out for snakes. I don't like snakes. There's no floor in this tent. They could crawl right in with us." Anita said, "We might want to buy a tent with a floor in it for Mexican camping." Juanita said, "Yes, I think that a floor would be a good idea. It's lucky that we put down a tarp to cover the ground, or our sleeping bags would be dirty by now."

They sat around the stove and cooked marshmallows. They ate the marshmallows and then added more wood to the fire. The tent got so warm that they all stripped off their clothes. The light from the fire gleamed off their naked bodies. The men spread lotion all over the girl's young attractive bodies. Each couple engaged in hours of fun with different positions. They didn't crawl into the sleeping bags right away. They had their fun on top of the bags. Finally when they became excited enough, they crawled into the bags and had even more fun. They were making it likely that soon there would be children for them to enjoy."

Juanita said, "In Mexico most women want to have children. At first I didn't want any, but now that I have become so attached to you, Bill, I want to give you a child. The child will remind me of you when you are away." Bill said, "In sixteen years, I will be able to draw social security. Then I might spend much more time in Mexico. American money goes further there." Juanita said, "I am looking forward to that." Jeff said, "It would be nice to retire in Mexico. We would have plenty of money then for living expenses and for fishing and camping trips. If Anita gives me a child, I may be tempted to stay in Mexico some day."

The girls made some coffee and they got dressed. Everyone took their coffee down by the edge of the water. They sat on a log and watched the stars and moon. Juanita said, "Why won't you divorce your wife, Bill? You know that I love you." Bill said, "I just feel like it would be mean. She has been faithful to me. It would hurt her." Juanita said, "She might want you to leave her if she knew you were with me." Bill said, "You might be right. I just need to think about it longer. I don't want to make a snap decision about something this important." Juanita said, "I will wait. I know you will come live with me sometime." The couple got up and walked down the beach together holding hands.

Anita said, "I was thinking the same thing. Will you ever leave your wife to stay with me? Jeff said, "If I did, you would need to stop being sexual with the tourists. Where would our money come from?" Anita said, "I make good money from the fishing charter even if I don't do sexual favors for the clients. I would promise to be loyal to you. You could work part time at the motel like we've planned." Jeff said, "I'm like Bill. I don't want to be mean to my wife when she's done nothing to deserve that." Anita said, "But you told me that she doesn't try hard to be sexually pleasing. Didn't you say that?" Jeff said, "I just haven't gotten used to the idea of divorce. She probably would want me to leave if she knew I was with you. I will leave her sometime. I just can't tell you when, yet." Anita said, "That is enough for me, as long as you promise to come live with me while our child is still young." Jeff said, "I won't make you wait more than five years. That will give me time to adjust to the idea. Every seventh year, you and I will need to live in the States for a year. That way I won't lose my citizenship and social security." Anita said, "That will be fine with me. We can rent an apartment next to Bill and Juanita. We could spend the year camping and fishing in the States. It would be fun."

Jeff said, "I want to show you the state of Michigan. They have black bears in the northern most regions. The fishing in

Lake Michigan is great. There are plenty of lake trout and salmon that weigh over 20 pounds. That state has lots of protected forests to camp in. There are many fine lakes all over the state. It is fun to see the many light houses that are along the shorelines." Anita said, "It sounds like a wonderful place. I can't wait to see it." Jeff said, "When I was a young boy, my grandfather used to take me to Pine Lake, near Marcellus, Michigan. We usually caught 20 to 40 nice sized bluegill when we went fishing there. My grandfather had me skin the fish with a rotary fish skinner. He would cut off the heads, remove the guts, and cut off the fins. We went almost every week in the summer. I got so that I could tell just when a fish was about to bite. It was some sort of sixth sense I think. My grandmother knew how to cook the fish just right. She breaded them in white flower and corn meal, and cooked them in butter. We always ate the fish on buttered bread. We never filleted the fish. My grandparents didn't want to loose any of the meat from the rib cage. We all loved to eat the fish eggs that were in the fish in the spring time. We fried them right along with the fish. I often drive by that lake so that I can remember my grandparents. They died about 16 years ago. They were wonderful people."

Anita and Jeff walked along the beach holding hands. After about an hour they met Juanita and Bill. Anita said, "We should all plan on marrying in five years from now. We could buy houses next to each other. Our children could play together." Bill said, "That sounds like a reasonable goal. But both of you have to remember to keep the sex good. If you get lazy like our wives, we'll trade you in for younger models." Juanita laughed and said, "And we would deserve it. I will always try to be exciting to you, Bill." Anita said, "And I will stay exciting. Sex is not just a duty for me. I always want it to be fun and exciting." Jeff said, "That sounds good to me. I don't want any more divorces."

They walked back to the tent and added more wood to the fire in the stove. Juanita made some more coffee. They all drank coffee and played cards till late. Then they got into the sleeping bags and slept naked. They were tired and fell asleep right away. The next morning they woke early to the sounds of waves and seagulls. They decided to call the charter service and go back to Anchorage. Juanita said, "I have heard so much about salmon in America. I would like to catch some of them." Jeff said, "They have nice big salmon in Alaska. We can fish for king salmon and Arctic char." He got out his maps of Alaska and found a good river. Then he located a town near the ocean that was also on the river. He said, "Here is a nice location. Alakanuk is at the mouth of the Yukon River. There is bound to be good fishing there. It is close enough to the ocean that we can fish there too if we want to." Anita said, "It sounds good to me, but where could we pitch the tent?" Jeff said, "If there isn't anywhere to camp, we can rent a cabin. There are always cabins for rent." Juanita said, "That sounds good to me. I've never stayed in a cabin."

They went to the trading post and called the plane charter. The company said they would pick them up in about an hour. They went back to the beach and got the tent and stove ready for the flight. When everything was ready, they went back to the trading post and drank coffee till they saw the planes arrive. They ran to the pier and got on the planes. Jeff had called and arranged for the pilots to fly them to Alakanuk. The planes were loaded and they took off. It was a clear day and the sun was shining. They all watched the scenery as the planes headed west towards the western cost of Alaska. In three hours they were landing on the Yukon River outside of Alakanuk. The pilots unloaded their gear on the pier. Jeff paid them and then went into town and hired a fishing guide. The man's name was Jim Andrews. He was about 60 years old and had gray hair and a beard. He was 6 feet tall and thin. Jim wore old blue jeans and a flannel shirt.

He drove his Chevy van to the pier and loaded up the tent and camping equipment. They all got in with him and he drove them to a private camp site near the ocean. He said, "You'll have privacy here. When would you like to go fishing?" Jeff said, "We'd like to start at 6:00 o'clock in the morning. We didn't bring any rods for the girls." Jim said, "I have a couple they can use. The salmon are running well this week. You came at the right time."

Jeff said, "Good, we'd like to catch some char too." Jim said, "There are plenty of them. I'll go along on the first day to make sure you get dialed in on how to catch plenty of fish." Jeff said, "Are there any cabins for rent on the river near town. The girls have never stayed in a cabin before." Jim said, "I have one to rent out by the ocean. It's only $20 a night." Jeff said, "What is today?" Jim said, "This is Monday." Jeff said, "We'd like to rent it on Wednesday." Jim said, "That'll be acceptable. Is one of the ladies your wife?" Jeff said, "No, we're engaged." Jim said, "Don't worry. I'm not concerned about whether you're married or not. That is, I'll rent the cabin to you. I was just curious." Jeff said, "I understand. This is Anita Fernandez my wife to be." Bill said, "I'm Bill Ellis and this is Juanita Rojas my wife to be." Jim shook all their hands. He said, "We don't see women this beautiful here in Alakanuk."

Jim helped the men put up the tent and installed the stove. Then he said, "I'll bring you some fire wood." He drove away and they all walked along the river. Not far away the river opened onto the Pacific Ocean. They walked along the ocean beach and watched the seagulls. The sun was nice and warm. Juanita said, "I wish we had a blanket. We could sun bath." Jeff said, "It doesn't feel quite that warm to me." They walked back to the tent and found a large pile of wood that was split small for wood stove use. They started the fire in the stove and made some coffee. After about an hour, Jim returned and offered to take them for a boat ride. Jeff said, "I think we would all like a river trip."

They climbed into the van and went to a pier next to Jim's house. He led them to the boat and everyone climbed in. It was a 31 foot cabin cruiser. The exterior was completely white and immaculately clean. Jim steered the boat upriver and went about 10 m.p.h. Anita asked Jim, "How do you fish for king salmon?" Jim said, "When the salmon head upstream, they aren't really interested in food. They are going as far as they can upstream to reproduce. The salmon only bite a lure when it is right in front of them. They are just angry at the lure. They aren't trying to eat it. Often they swim across the line and get it in their mouth. The fisherman feels the tug and slides the line through the salmon's mouth until the lure comes up and snags the salmon. Snagging is not legal, but when the snagging is in the mouth, it is sometimes hard to say what is legal and what is not." Anita said, "I'd rather catch fish that are hungry and bite the lure. Do char bite the lure?" Jim said, "Yes, you will like char fishing. They aren't as big as king salmon, but there are plenty of them and they are fun to catch."

They went upstream for several hours and saw some grizzly bears along the bank. They had fish they were eating. They looked up as the boat went by. The boat didn't bother them. The girls watched closely and took some pictures. Next they saw a large moose crossing the river. Its antlers were impressive as it swam with surprising speed to the other side of the river. There were Indians in canoes spear fishing and using nets. Juanita said, "I've never seen anything like this. Where will we fish in the morning?" Jim said, "Anywhere along the bank is good. Most of the fish stay close to the bank. We can fish right at your campsite if you like. The char can be found anywhere in the river. We can fish from the boat for them. I will take you to many different spots to fish for them."

They started to see dozens of grizzly bears and brown bears. All of them were fishing along the bank for salmon. They looked up as the boat went by. Anita asked, "Where is the next town on the river?" Jim said, "That would be Mountain Village. It's about 100 miles upstream. We won't be going that far. Fuel is too expensive. Besides it would take all day to get there." Anita said, "So most travel is by plane then?" Jim said, "Yes, it is the main way people get around. Most people don't travel much. It's too expensive for the average person." Jim said, "I'm going to take the boat over close to the bank. If you watch closely you will see the salmon swimming upstream." He steered over to the bank and went slowly along side the bank. They all looked into the water. There were the large king salmon and other fish swimming along the bottom. They showed up well in the 6 foot deep water.

Jeff said, "What is there to catch out on the ocean?" Jim said, "We can fish for halibut and flounder. Sometimes you get surprised about what you catch on the ocean. I can't tell you exactly what we might catch." Jeff said, "We will probably fish the river for a couple days, and then spend a day on the ocean if the weather is calm enough." Jim said, "That'll be fine for me. You might want to go out on the ocean the first day that it's calm enough." Jeff said, "That's right. We have to work with the weather." They watched the shore line and noticed that it was thick with pine trees and white birch. There were a few grassy areas, but most of the area was wooded. There were many ducks and geese on the river. Song birds sang from the edge of the river.

Juanita said, "We would really like to go in your boat to Mountain Village. If we pay for the gas and your time, will you take us there? It would be a great adventure for us." Jim said, "Well if you have your heart set on it, I could take you. My boat has an oversized gas tank. It holds 100 gallons. I could refuel when we get to Mountain Village. You will see mostly what you've seen already; wildlife, water and lots of trees." Juanita said, "I like the isolation. I've never been a long way from towns, except for the last two days when we've been at the Katmai Park." Jim said, "I've never been to that park. What's it like?" Juanita said, "The only building where we camped was a trading post. There was a toilet, but no shower. It was more primitive than Alakanuk. I'm hoping that you have a shower that we can use." Jim said, "You can all use the shower at my house. There is no shower with the cabin you'll be staying in. Just come over whenever you want to use it. I don't mind the intrusions. I get bored here in this little village. It will be nice to have someone new to talk to. I only do charters during the summer months. The rest of the year gets pretty boring. We play bingo a lot, and poker." By the way, if any of you need to use the toilet, this boat has a head." Juanita said, "What is the head on a boat?" Jim said, "It is the nautical term for toilet. It is down the stairs and to the left." Juanita said, "That's good to know. We may want to use the head. Can we look around in the cabin?" Jim said, "You can go on down and look around." The girls led the men down the stairs to the boat's small kitchen.

They turned left and peaked in at the head. It was tidy and looked clean. There was even a small shower in the head.

On past the kitchen was the last room. It was wall to wall bed. The girls giggled and Anita said, "I wonder if he would rent us his boat for a night?" Jeff said, "I'm sure he would for a price. I'll ask him." Juanita said, "I think it would be fun to stay on the boat for a night. I'll pay him. He certainly won't want more than $100. It would be one of the most memorable parts of our trip." Jeff said, "You can give me the money. I'll negotiate with him." Juanita said, "That would be the best. Here's the money." She handed him five twenty dollar bills. Jeff said, "I'll give you the change. He went back to the main deck and talked with Jim. He said, "Would you let us rent your boat for one night. Just to stay in it and eat in the kitchen. We've never been on a boat like this one." Jim said, "For $80 dollars you can have it all day and all night. Just promise to be careful with everything. I try to keep her ship shape." Jeff said, "We'll take good care of her. You can leave it at the pier. We don't want to take it anywhere." Jim said, "That sounds good. You wouldn't want to risk being washed down stream while you sleep. The current here is rather swift." Jeff gave him the $80 and said, "Can you fill the refrigerator with bacon, eggs and bread? We have coffee. If you have a six pack of beer we would like that too. Keep track of the expense and we'll pay you. We'd like to stay on the boat tomorrow night." Jim said, "I'll have everything ready for you. This boat has little heat. You will want to bring your sleeping bags." Jeff said, "We have some nice warm ones."

The girls and Bill came up from the galley and listened to Jeff. He said, "We'll stay here tomorrow night. We can use our sleeping bags. There's not much heat on the boat. The next night we will stay in the cabin, and then we will go up river to see Mountain Village." Bill said, "It sounds like a busy week. It will be fun." Juanita said to Anita, "Won't it be fun?" Anita said, "It will be wonderful. I can't wait to get started." Jim said, "Shall we head on back now. We can get back in time to have supper before sunset." Jeff said, "Why don't you have supper with us at the campsite? We would like to talk to you some more." Jim said, "I'd be glad to join you. I have plenty of char in my freezer. Believe it or not I have a microwave oven. I can thaw the fish out quickly and we can cook them over an open fire." Anita said, "That sounds good. We can heat coffee on our stove in the tent." Jim said, "I'll bring some beer in a cooler full of ice. I hope Coors light is O.K. That's about all I drink." Jeff said, "We like Coors. Add the beer to our bill. We don't want you to have to pay for our beer. Your rates here are reasonable." Jim said, "O.K. I'll keep track of everything. Just tell me if there is anything else you want."

Jim turned the boat around and headed back to his pier. In about an hour and a half they arrived at Jim's house. Jeff and Bill helped dock the boat. Juanita and Anita were still admiring the scenery. Jim took them to his house and filled a cooler with ice and beer. While Jim thawed out the char, Anita and Juanita looked around the house. The men stayed in the kitchen and talked with Jim. The girls went to the dining room first. There was an antique hutch and an old oak table. There were kerosene lamps everywhere. The windows were small and not overly attractive. Juanita said, "You have a nice cozy house here, Jim." Jim said, "Thanks. It gets me by. I like it." They went on into the dining room. It was large and had a black bear rug on the floor in front of a large fire place. There were several kerosene lanterns in the living room too. Juanita went to the kitchen and asked Jim, "Why so many kerosene lamps? You have electric lights." Jim said, "I like the kerosene lamps. Sometimes the town generator goes down. Then it's handy to have the kerosene lamps." The girls noticed that the kitchen stove had a chimney. Anita said, "Do you cook with wood?" Jim said, "Yes, sometimes we run out of propane here. Wood is always available."

The girls went out in the yard and walked around the house. It was dark brown with wooden siding. The roof was made of tin. Jim must not have owned a lawn mower. His yard looked just like the rest of the woods around it. He lived about a quarter mile from town, to the east of it. Soon Jim appeared at the front door with the cooler. He said, "The fish are ready, we can go." They all crawled into the van and rode with Jim to their camp site.

It was about an hour till sunset when they started cooking the fish on a fire Jim built. The fish sizzled in butter as they slowly cooked. Jim got out a beer for each of them. They all sat on logs around the fire and watched the fish cooking. Jim said, "What do you and Bill do for a living, Jeff?" Jeff said, "We both retired early. My wife works as an English teacher, and Bill's wife works part time as an interior decorator. "Jim said, "Juanita, do you and Anita work?" Juanita said, "We are charter fishing guides just like you." Jim said, "That's amazing. How much do you get for a days charter?" Juanita said, "We charge $450 for four days of fishing. That includes both of us and our boat captain. It also includes food, lodging and beer. We are located in Loreto, Mexico. Everything is less expensive in Mexico." Jim said, "It sounds like it. I'm tempted to sign up for a charter for this winter. It gets pretty boring here in the winter. Nobody comes here for charters then. The weather is too bad. Everything is frozen. It gets down to minus 60 degrees here in January." Juanita said, "It would be a good time for you to come and stay with us. We'll treat you very well."

Jim said, "Possibly I could drive my boat to Mexico. Where is Loreto?" Juanita said, "It is on the east side of the Baja Peninsula. We can draw you a map. If you come, we will let you take fishermen out fishing. You could work for our boss for the winter." Jim said, "I was just pipe dreaming. I would miss this town too much. It's where my wife and I lived together before she died. A grizzly bear killed her while she was fishing from the bank just east of town a couple miles. That's why I usually have my clients fish from the boat. It's safer." Juanita said, "I'm sorry to hear about your wife. Do you think you will ever marry again?" Jim said, "I don't think so. I'm used to being alone. I have friends here in Alakunuk. We play cards and fish together. That's all I need."

The fish were finally done and Jim served them on paper plates. Everyone grabbed another beer and they ate fish with beer. It was getting dark. Juanita said, "I'd like a shower tonight,

Jim. Do you mind driving me to your place for a shower, and then bring me back. Jim said, "I don't mind at all." Anita said, "I could use a shower too." Jeff said, "I'd like to stay here and watch the sunset." Bill said, "I'll stay here with Jeff. You girls hurry back. We'll be getting up early." Juanita said, "Don't worry we'll come right back." Jim led the way to his van and took the girls back to his house. When they got in the house Anita said, "You can watch us shower if you'd like. We aren't married yet. I like you and I'd like for you to watch us." Jim said, "I'll peek in for a little while, I guess. You are both very attractive women." Anita and Juanita giggled and went into the bathroom. They stripped and got into the shower. They took a real hot shower, and the steam started filling the room.

Jim came in and watched them wash themselves. He said, "Don't tell Jeff and Bill that I was watching you shower, O.K?" Juanita said, "Don't worry. We won't tell them. But they wouldn't care anyway. They know that we get pretty physical with the tourists in Loreto. We do it to get tips. We need the money." Jim said, "You could make lots of money in Fairbanks giving massages and getting physical with the customers. You could probably make $3,000 a day." Anita said, "Would you be our manager?" Jim said, "I'd be glad to. Just give me 20 percent of what you take in. I'm not greedy." Juanita said, "That's a generous offer. I think we would stay here during the winter when there aren't many tourists fishing in Loreto. We could make enough in three months to retire." Jim said, "Yes, you could. When your men decide to marry you, you could retire with them in style. You could see the world. You girls look terribly beautiful. You could charge men to watch you shower. In the winter here, there is not enough entertainment. The men would love you two."

Juanita said, "I don't think we should discuss this with Jeff and Bill. They will find out this winter when we aren't in Loreto. We'll have to tell them then. I'll give you our phone number. You can set up a place for us in Fairbanks for the beginning of November. Make sure there is a hot tub and shower for us to entertain the men in. We might even let men in the shower with us if they promised to behave. We could charge another $100 for that." Jim said, "You think like a business woman." Jim said, "Do you mind if I join you in the shower? Anita said, "Now that we are business partners, I think we can trust you." He stripped and got into the shower with them. It was pretty crowded in there. The girls pressed up against him and rubbed their breasts all over him. He said, "This is worth several hundred dollars for 20 minutes. The men here are willing to spend plenty on pretty women."

Finally they ran out of hot water. They dried off and got dressed. Jim said, "You girls really know how to make a man feel like a man. I can see why Bill and Jeff want to marry you." Juanita said, "Yes, if we can ever get them to leave their wives. Their wives aren't sexually satisfying compared to us, but they're both dragging their feet." Jim said, "It isn't nice to start a divorce. It seems like a mean thing to do. Feelings get hurt." Anita said, "Yes, but to intentionally be less than pleasing to your husband, isn't that asking for trouble?" Jim said, "Well, their wives are causing Jeff and Bill to be easy prey for temptation. Not only are you two very attractive and young, it sounds like you believe in making your man completely pleased sexually." Anita said, "That is what makes me feel like a real woman." Juanita said, "I like to see just how turned on I can make Bill get." Jim said, "I don't think you will have any trouble winning your men and keeping them." Anita said, "I hope you're right. They sure are dragging their feet. At least we can use this foot dragging time to make some good money."

They went outside and climbed into the van. Jim drove them back to the camp site. The girls climbed out and Jim waved to the men and drove away. Juanita said, "I'd like to go right to bed. We'll be getting up early in the morning." Anita said, "Me too. Let's get some sleep. They built up the fire in the wood stove and then everyone climbed into the sleeping bags. They fell asleep quickly after some good night kissing.

At 5:00 o'clock in the morning everyone was wakened by the sound of a bear outside the tent. Jeff went to the door and peeked out. The bear was licking the ground where some butter had been spilled from the frying pan. The bear had smelled the fried fish and butter mixture, and came to investigate. They were lucky they had no food in the tent. Jeff rattled the coffee pot loudly on the stove and shouted loudly. When he peeked out again the bear was still there. Everyone got dressed and tried to think what to do. They didn't even have a pocket knife to fight the bear if it attacked. They all went to the door of the tent and yelled loudly at the bear. It turned and moved towards them. It rose up on its hind feet and walked close to the door of the tent. It growled ferociously and showed its teeth.

Suddenly a shot rang out and the bear fell to the ground. Jim drove up in his van. He said, "It's lucky I always keep my rifle in the van. I was coming to see if you were all waking up on time to go fishing this morning. It looked like that bear was being a little troublesome, so I shot it for you. I can have it skinned for you if you'd like. It would make a nice rug. That's a brown bear. He must have liked the smell of those fish we cooked last night." Jeff said, "We're glad you came when you did. We didn't know what to do. We don't have any weapons.

Jim said, "I can fix that. After we fish, I'll take you to the trading post and you can each buy a big knife. You need one up here. At least you'd have a chance against a bear. You could buy a couple rifles too if you want to." Jeff said, "I think a rifle would be an excellent idea. What kind would you recommend?" Jim said, "I think that a Remington 30-06 would stop any bear. When it comes to protecting your life, you don't want to skimp." Jeff said, "I agree. How much are they?" Jim said, "You can get a good used one for around $300. A new one could cost $600 or more." Jeff said, "I'm looking forward to our visit to the trading post. Would they have any 45 caliber semi-auto hand guns?" Jim said, "They have plenty of them, but you would have to wait awhile before you could pick it up. They have to do a background check." Jeff said, "I have a carry permit. I could take the gun with me right away." Jim said, "We'll have to ask about that at the trading post. I don't think your Indiana permit would be valid in

Alaska. If it isn't valid, a rifle will make excellent protection. They are legal without any special permit."

Juanita and Anita built up the fire and put some coffee on. They also cooked some bacon and eggs. The men built up the campfire, and everyone had breakfast around the fire. Jim said, "We can fish here from the bank or I can take you out in the boat, whichever you prefer." Bill said, "I think I would rather fish from the boat. There would be fewer things to get tangled up in. The grass is pretty thick along the bank." Jim said, "That's a good point. The boat it is, then." They finished breakfast and climbed into the van. After arriving at Jim's house, they helped him carry the fishing rods and tackle from the van to the boat. Jeff asked, "Are king salmon very good to eat?" Jim said, "The younger smaller ones aren't bad. The big old ones are a little strong flavored." Bill asked, "What about the Arctic char? Are they good to eat?" Jim said, "They are good, whether they are big or small."

Juanita said, "Will Anita and I be able to catch king salmon? How big are they?" Jim said, "You can both fish for them. If you hook an 80 pounder that is too large for you to handle, we can help you. Don't worry about a thing. Just don't let go of your rod. I don't want to loose any of them. Should I call the owner of the trading post and have him skin out that bear for a rug?" Juanita said, "I would like it for my room in the motel at Loreto." Anita said, "I would like one too." Jim said, "When Jeff gets his rifle we can hunt another bear. I'm sure another one will come around the campsite. It just surprised me that they moved in so soon. I'll go call the trading post. Old Bob Miller will be glad to skin out that bear and tan it for you. You can all make yourselves at home on the boat. I'll be back in about 10 minutes." Jim left quickly and headed for the house.

The girls went to the galley and snooped through the cupboards. They found cereal, canned tuna, sardines, crackers and a bottle of Jack Daniels. There were plenty of glasses and plates. They opened a can of sardines and poured everyone some whiskey. Juanita said, "I've never had sardines before." She bit into one and made a funny face. She said, "Maybe these are emergency rations. I can't imagine anyone liking these things." She quickly washed it down with some whiskey. Jeff said, "I like them." He put some between a couple crackers and ate them eagerly. Bill tried them and said, "I think they're good." Finally Anita ate one. She said, "I don't think they are too bad." She put some between crackers and ate them. They all washed the sardines down with whiskey.

Soon Jim returned. He was pleased to see they had made themselves at home. He said, "Help yourselves to anything you see there. I have plenty more whiskey on the boat. Just don't get too drunk to fish. We can drink more at the end of the day." He laughed and poured himself a drink. Then he untied the boat and started the engine. The boat moved smoothly downstream to the mouth of the river. Jim told his fishermen, "The fish are most concentrated at the mouth of the river at this time. They are staging there, getting ready to head on upstream. Of course some have already gone upstream. You saw them yesterday moving along the bank. There are also many fish moving out in the middle of the river. I think we should fish out just past the mouth of the river. That is where the fish are most concentrated. There will be native fishermen there in their small boats. There aren't as many commercial fishermen here as there are farther south. Expenses are too high here. We are a long ways from civilization. Everything has to be flown in."

In no time they were at the mouth of the Yukon River. Jim anchored the boat and rigged up the lines. He had them fish with spawn bags on number 10 treble hooks. They cast across the current and reeled slowly back towards the boat. It wasn't long till Anita hooked a fish. She said, "Oh, it feels like a big one!" She cranked in the line with a pumping action on the rod. She brought the rod up to 12:00 o'clock and then cranked quickly down to the 3:00 o'clock position. Over and over she repeated the process. She strained noticeably as she cranked the rod. She had a big fish alright. After about 25 minutes she pulled the king salmon along side of the boat. Jim netted it for her. He hoisted the large red fish onto the deck. He said, "This one must weight 60 pounds! It's a nice large king. He placed it in the cooler full of ice. It was big enough that its tail stuck out of the cooler.

After they had fished for 8 hours, each fisherman had a 60 pound or larger king salmon. They had several smaller ones too that would be the best to eat. Jim switched the bait to a silver and blue spoon. They started fishing for Arctic char. It wasn't long until they each had several of these nice fish. Jim said, "We can have a real cook out tonight. It should lure in plenty of bears. We'd better leave now so that we can shop at the trading post while it is open." Jim hoisted up the anchor and the headed back to the pier. He said, "I have electricity to my pier that will light the boat tonight when you sleep on it. I'll bring over your sleeping bags while you look around in the trading post." Jeff said, "That'll be great. When can we shoot a bear?" Jim said, "Get yourself a license at the trading post. You can shoot one Wednesday morning probably. This is Tuesday, and they will be out eating our fish scraps. We can leave some fish around just to tempt them." Jeff said, "I'll help you carry the cooler." Jim said, "Thanks. That will be a big help." They carried the cooler full of fish up to Jim's cleaning station on the bank. Jim strung up the fish and took pictures of the fish and fishermen with Jeff's camera. Then he cleaned the fish in just a short time. He was quite skilled with a fillet knife.

Next he drove them to the trading post. The trading post was a log building with a stove pipe coming out the top. It measured about 40 feet wide and 60 feet long. Jim introduced them all to Bob Miller, the proprietor. Bob was an old man with a full gray beard. He was short and fat, with blue eyes and large hands and feet. Bob said, "I'm glad to meet all of you. Feel free to look around. I'll be glad to answer any questions you may have." Jeff asked, "How much is a bear hunting license?" Bob asked, "Are you out of state?" Jeff said, "Yes, I'm from Indiana." Bob said, "That license is $100." Jeff said, "I'll take one, and I'd like to look at Remington 30-06 rifles." Bob said, "I have several used and new one. Let me show you them now." He led Jeff to the back of the trading post. Lined up in a row were the rifles. The price was on each gun. Jeff looked at them carefully. Finally he said, "Which would you recommend?" Bob said, "If you can afford it, buy a new rifle. It makes you feel good to own something that nice. The used ones are in perfect condition, though. They would be a good buy also." Jeff looked at the rifles for a long time, while the others looked around the store.

Juanita and Anita were looking at wool pants and long underwear. The weather was still quite cool early in the morning. Their warm coats were adequate, but the girls were used to being warm in Mexico. There was frost on the grass in the morning. Juanita and Anita each bought long underwear and pants large enough to wear over them. They also bought some thermal socks and boots large enough to fit over them. Bill bought a large hunting knife and a compass. He also bought long underwear and pants big enough to wear over them. He went to tell Jeff about the long underwear. He said, "Jeff, you'll want to buy long underwear. It's pretty cold up here." But Jeff was too busy looking at guns. He said, "I think I'll buy this used rifle. It's like new and it's semi-auto. I like the idea of getting a quick second shot." Bill said, "I agree. You'll save money, and it is a perfectly good gun."

Jeff took the gun and some ammo to the cash register and laid them on the counter. He bought his bear hunting license and then looked at the long underwear. He bought a pair, and a pair of pants that would fit over them. He also bought thermal socks and some heavy water proof boots. They sat at a table and drank coffee until Jim returned with the van. Jeff thought of one more thing to buy. He bought several topographical maps of the area. He said, "I just like to look at them. They include everything. Every hill and stream. Every path."

The group left the trading post and got into Jim's van. He took them to the campsite, where the girls started the fire in the stove and the men started the campfire. Soon the girls served coffee. They all sat around the fire and told fishing stories till the sun went down. They cooked up a big mess of fish and ate them with bread and butter. Jim intentionally left scraps of bread and drippings from the skillet around the fire to attract bears. When they had finished eating, Jim drove them all to his boat. He had left the lights on in the boat, and took them on a tour of it, showing them where all the light switches were. He said, "There's plenty of hot water for showers. There is a heating element in the hot water line. It heats the water as fast as you use it. That way you never run out of water and it saves room. There's no big water heater to take up space. There are two electric heaters. One is under the table in the galley, and the other is in the sleeping quarters. They keep the boat from getting real cold, but you'll be glad you have your sleeping bags." Jim pulled another bottle of Jack Daniels from the refrigerator. He said, "Shall we all have another drink before I leave?" Jeff said, "It sounds like a good idea to me." They all sat around the table in the galley and drank whiskey. Finally after several rounds, Jim said, "I have to go to the house and get some sleep. You can all come to the house in the morning and have ham and eggs." Bill said, "We'll be there." Jim climbed up the stairs to the main deck and disappeared. Juanita said, "I get the shower first." Bill said, "I'll share it with you." Juanita said, "If there's room. It's kind of small." Bill said, "I like a cozy shower." They stripped and got into the shower. Anita dug through some drawers and found the towels. She put a couple in the bathroom with Juanita and Bill. The steam was already forming in the air. Bill and Juanita had been embracing under the stream of hot water. Anita was envious and couldn't wait until she and Jeff would get their turn under the hot water.

Jeff and Anita played some cards while they waited on the shower. Juanita was giving Bill the presidential treatment under the hot water. She enjoyed the novelty of the little bathroom. After about 20 minutes of that ecstasy for Bill, Juanita let Bill guide her into a new position for them. It was a little difficult in the tight spaces of the little shower, but they managed. She moaned softly as he got more forceful just before he reached the peak of his excitement. Anita heard the moaning and peeked in at them. When she saw what they were doing, she made up her mind to do it with Jeff. She quietly closed the door without letting them know that she had peeked in on them.

She went back to Jeff and told him what they were doing. He could feel himself start to get excited about what Anita wanted. He held her hand and told her how much he was wanting her. They passed the time waiting for the shower, by kissing passionately and rubbing each other in intimate spots. Finally, Bill and Juanita came out of the shower. They were wrapped in towels, and headed for the bedroom. Jeff and Anita stripped and hurried into the shower. They enjoyed the new position for the day. Since they were the last to use the shower, they took their time and tried a few extra things under the nice hot water. They were very creative, and didn't want to leave the shower without having used it to its fullest potential.

Finally they turned off the shower and dried off. They went to the bedroom and crawled into their sleeping bag. Juanita said, "We could feel the boat rocking while you two were in the shower. What were you doing?" Then she giggled. Anita said, "We were being creative." Jeff said, "Showers are wonderful things, aren't they?" Bill said, "Yes, they are great." Everyone was a little exhausted from their fun. They fell asleep quickly in the warm sleeping bags. The men loved the feel of the young naked women cuddling up close to them.

Early in the morning Jim woke them. He said, "It's time for breakfast. I have everything ready. We need to go to your campsite and shoot a bear." All the boat people got dressed quickly and hurried up to Jim's cabin. They had worked up an appetite. He had plenty of ham and eggs waiting for them. There was also some nice strong coffee. They had cinnamon toast with the breakfast, and orange juice. There was a fire in the wood fueled cook stove in Jim's kitchen. Everything was nice and warm. Jeff said, "I'll go load the rifle. I won't chamber a shell till we see a bear." Jim said, "That's the way I would do it. It's safer."

They all finished their breakfast and then hopped into the van and headed to the campsite. They stopped two hundred yards back and watched as two large brown bears rooted through the

ashes and ate scraps of fish. Jeff rested the rifle on the vans
window and aimed through the iron sites of the rifle. He shot and
one bear fell to the ground. The other bears took off running to
the northwest. They waited for awhile to make sure the bear was
dead. Then they drove up and had a closer look. It was truly a
large brown bear. Jeff said, "It'll make a great bear rug." He had
Jim take a picture of him and his gun with the bear. Then he had
Jim get a picture of Bill with him and the bear. Then there was a
picture of Anita and Juanita with the bear. Last of all a picture of
all the men and women with the bear. Anita and Juanita gave Jim
their address so that he could ship the rugs to their motel.

Jim took them to the cabin they would be staying in the next
night. It was facing the ocean. The sea gulls were crying as they
walked up to the small log cabin. It only had single beds, but
there was a nice large fireplace that looked inviting. There were
several bear rugs on the floor. There was a stove and a table and
chairs. The cabin had plenty of windows that faced the ocean.
Jim said, "You can stay here as long as you like. I'll let you have
it for half price. You can leave the tent up and stay in it any time
you like. Jeff said, "Thanks Jim. We'll probably stay here a couple
days. Can you take us up the river today?" Jim said, "That's fine
with me. The boat is full of gas and there's plenty of food on
board. I'll buy a couple more bottles of whiskey and we'll be
ready to go." Jim drove them back to the boat and left them there
while he went to town for the whiskey.

Juanita, Anita, Bill and Jeff climbed down into the galley
and poured themselves some Jack Daniels. They ate crackers
with the whiskey. By the time they had finished the first couple
rounds, Jim was back with the extra whisky. He put two fifths in
the refrigerator. Next he untied the boat and started the motor.
He pulled away from the pier and steered upstream. Everyone
went to the main deck and sat in lawn chairs. They watched the
trees go by and looked at the wildlife. They discussed where to
go next. Juanita said, "I'd like to see the town you live in, Bill."
Bill said, "I don't want to risk having my wife see us, or someone
I know. We could go to a town nearby." Juanita said, "We can

drive by at night. That would be fine, wouldn't it?" Bill said, "That's fine. We can fish on Lake Michigan." Jeff said, "Yes, we can catch some nice lake trout this time of year. We can stay in Grand Haven. That is where the best charter boats are."

Jim said, "We'll be at Mountain Village in about 4 or 5 hours. What do you want to do there?" Anita said, "I'd like to go to the trading post and look around." Jim said, "That's fine. They have a nice trading post. We could tour one of the old gold mines." Anita said, "I would like that." Juanita said, "Maybe we could find some gold." Jim said, "We could pan for gold if you want to. There is still gold to be found. Just not as much as there used to be." Bill said, "I would like to pan for gold. Do we get to keep the gold?" Jim said, "You get to keep everything that you find. They charge so much per day to pan. I don't know how much it is."

A little after noon they arrived in Mountain Village. Jim docked the boat and they walked through town. It was a small town, much like Alakanuk. Jim led them to the trading post. They each bought a coffee cup with the town name and information about the town on it. Anita bought a bag of hard candy. It was butterscotch flavored. Juanita bought some Vicks cough drops. They sat in the store for awhile and drank coffee. Juanita said, "Sometime when there is more time, I'd like to take the boat all the way to Fairbanks if the river goes that far." Jim said, "The river goes that far, but it would take several weeks by boat." Juanita said, "That's what I had in mind. Oh, Jim, would you show me the thermal socks." Jim led her through the store. Juanita said, "I just wanted to get you away from the others so that I could talk to you alone. Don't you think we could run the massage parlor out of the boat? It would save us rent." Jim said, "During the winter the river is frozen solid. I have to take the boat out of the water in the winter. I'll find us an inexpensive place for the massage parlor, and a place where we can live too. Those expenses will be minimal compared to the thousands of dollars we'll be taking in." Juanita said, "I suppose you're right. We'd better get back to the others so they don't get suspicious."

Jim and Juanita joined the others. They finished their coffee and rented a car from the town barber. He let them have it for $20. They drove around until they found the gold mining outfit. They panned for gold most of the day and each found a couple nice nuggets. They drove back to town and gave the car back to the barber. Next they had a tasty chicken dinner at the local restaurant. Juanita said, "I thought this town would be a little more exciting. What do people do for excitement in this town?" Jim said, "Most people trap for hides or take people hunting. When they come to town for supplies they drink and chase women. There aren't too many women in this town, so don't be surprised if the men really look you over. Shall we go into the tavern?" Juanita said, "Sure, I'd like to see it." They had been drinking whiskey, so they ordered some more whiskey. There were 10 or 12 men in the place. They were all staring at the girls. One man came up and said, "My name is Jake and I'd like to buy you girls a drink." Anita said, "We already have a drink, but thank you very much." Jake said, "I'm a trapper and I don't get to see many pretty women. I'm out in the woods all the time." Juanita said, "You can buy us a drink, but don't expect anything. We're engaged to these two men." She introduced Jeff and Bill. Several other men came up. One said, "My name is Bart and I'd like to buy a drink for all of you."

The drinks started coming to the table. Soon everyone was buying everyone else drinks. Before they knew it the sun was setting. They asked the bar tender to make some hamburgers and fries. Anita left her phone number with the bar tender and whispered to him that in November they would be starting a massage parlor in Fairbanks. She whispered, "Juanita and I will be showering with the men and getting a little physical with them." The bar tender was visibly impressed. He said that he would spread the word. He asked, "Why are you whispering?" Anita said, "We don't want our boy friends to know yet. We're going to tell them later." The bar tender said, "My name is John. I'll keep quiet till you're gone. Then I'll tell the others. I want to be your first customer."

After they ate, they went back to the boat and drank some more whiskey. They played cards and ate sardines with crackers. The whiskey gave Anita the courage she needed to tell Jeff and Bill about the massage parlor idea. She said, "I have something to announce. In November Juanita and I are starting a massage parlor in Fairbanks. Jim will be our manager. We will shower with the men and get a little physical. No presidential treatment. After all we are engaged. We want to make $160,000 each in four months. Then we will have enough to retire on. In Mexico that is enough money to last for a lifetime." Jeff said, "That was quite a speech, Anita. I like your ambition, but after being with all those men in the shower, will you be in the mood to stay with just one man?" Anita said, "Of course I will. I only want to do it for the money. You are retired, and your wife will take half of everything when you divorce her. I don't think you have enough money to stay retired and also get a divorce. I am trying to make it so we can live together comfortably." Jeff said, "I don't object. We aren't married yet. You can do what you want to, but I don't think Bill and I will want to be around while you and Juanita are doing that sort of business. We would get jealous." Bill said, "Yes, it would mean that we couldn't be together for four months. But you're right, Anita. We don't have enough money to live on. It's smart thinking for you girls to make big money before we are married. I would love to live in Loreto. With that kind of money we could see the world together." Juanita said, "And it's not like we were going all the way with the men. There won't be any chance of us getting diseases, because we won't be doing things that cause the transfer of disease."

Bill said, "What if a man demands more and tries to rape one of you?" Anita said, "Jim will be close by with a stun gun. He will see that no one gets out of hand." Then she giggled and said, "No pun intended." Bill said, "If all you do is give special messages, I guess I would have no objection. You girls have experience with men. You will know how to keep them under control most of the time." Anita said, "We worked with lots of men last year on the charter boat. We had no manager to protect us, but we are still virgins." Jeff said, "Bill and I will just stay home from November till April. On April first, we will meet you in Loreto at the motel. It will be a wonderful reunion." Anita said, "You can call us in the morning when we aren't working. Get a cell phone. They don't cost too much. That way your wife won't find the calls listed on your home phone bill." Jeff said, "That's a good idea. I'll call often, and so will Bill." Bill said, "Sure, I can call that way."

They played cards till late at night, talking all the while about where they would travel to after they had all that money. Finally Jim said, "I'm getting a little tired. I think I'll go up on the deck with a blanket and take a nap." Jeff said, "We'll go to bed now. You can sleep here on the bench seat." Jim said, "Thanks, I'm used to sleeping here. You folks get a good night's sleep. We can sleep in late and then start our trip back to Alakanuk."

Jeff said, "Anita and I get the shower first." Jim said, "You are lucky that I was able to get electricity to the boat or it would have been a cold shower. They aren't used to boats docking here in Mountain Village." Jeff said, "I'm glad you're watching out for us, Jim." Jeff and Anita went to the bedroom and stripped for the shower. They came through the galley with only a towel around them. They got in the shower and hugged for a long time under the hot water. Anita gave Jeff the longest presidential treatment she had ever given anyone. They were both very fond of what they were doing, and went on for almost an hour. Jeff said, "I am very fond of you Anita. I love you." Anita said, "I love you too." She whispered in his ear, "You can have the presidential treatment anytime you want it. And I'll do it as long as you like. We can do more tonight if you like." Jeff said, "That would be great." They dried off and went to the bedroom. Anita whispered, "When we are married, I will still give it to you whenever you want. I won't get stingy like your wife." Jeff said, "That's reassuring. I really appreciate it. You won't regret it. I will try to make you happy." Anita switched off the light and said, "I will always try to make you happy. Just tell me what kind of sex you want. That is what you will get." She gave him as much pleasure as she knew how to give. She thought to herself, "I think I am winning him completely. He is mine now."

Juanita and Bill came to the bedroom to leave their clothes. They weren't shocked when they saw what Jeff and Anita were doing. They just removed their clothes and got towels to take to the shower. Jim came back and got another blanket. He too was not alarmed by what he saw. He laughed and said, "After they marry you, they don't want to do that anymore. Wedding cake has some ingredient that destroys sex drive." Then he laughed some more and went back to the galley. Anita stopped for a second and said, "Don't listen to him. I meant it. You can always have all you want. I swear." Then she went back to work on him. He stroked her hair fondly as she made him feel very good. Then she stopped again. She said, "I mustn't get pregnant until after this winter. We'll find many things we can do, but we need to be careful." Then she resumed her activity. Jeff said, "Well, if you aren't already pregnant, I think we can work to prevent it. If you are pregnant, you can put off the massage parlor work until the following winter." Anita nodded.

In the shower Juanita was hugging Bill and telling him what she was going to do to him. She could tell he was starting to get excited. He was poking her in the belly, but his hands were on her back. Slowly she slipped to her knees. She knew it was time for the presidential treatment. She had lots of experience, and was now trying to make him feel as good as possible. Bill spoke softly to her as she worked on him. She could feel his hands caressing her hair. Bill and Juanita went on like that for over an hour. Neither of them wanted to ever quit. Finally, they were fully sated for the moment. They dried off quickly and rushed to the bedroom. Once there, they resumed their activity. Occasionally they would change position so that the other could be on top. They went on for several hours there in the dark. Bill thought, "I sure will miss her this winter. She said, "I hope I'm not pregnant." Bill said, "You won't get pregnant this way." She laughed and said, "You know. I meant from when we went all the way in the tent. If I'm pregnant I'll have to wait a year to have the massage parlor." Bill said, "I don't think that just doing it a couple times will be likely to make you pregnant. We'll just have to wait and see." She said, "You're right. I'll know by next month."

Juanita grabbed a towel and wrapped it around herself. She went to the galley and got the bottle of whiskey off the table. She poured out some in a glass and drank it. She looked at Jim sleeping there on the bench. She smiled at him and then turned slowly and returned to the bedroom. She dropped the towel and crawled into the sleeping bag with Bill. She said, "Do you think you will divorce your wife soon?" Bill said, "It will be hard for me to break it to her. She is a nice woman and I hate to hurt her feelings. I will wait for Jeff to tell his wife. Then I will tell mine. The two wives will help each other get over it." Juanita said, "November would be a good time for Jeff to tell her. I don't want to wait five years." Bill said, "I'm sure it will be close to that time. You girls have a wonderful attitude towards sex. I don't want to take a chance on losing you. And Jeff doesn't want to lose Anita. We'll move ahead as fast as we can. If I had any doubts before, you erased them all tonight. I just want to be with you all the time." Juanita said, "That's wonderful of you to say. I will try to help you remember it." She put her arm around him and fell asleep with her breasts pressed tightly up against his back.

Early in the morning Juanita heard Anita shuffling around in the sleeping bag. She could faintly see the sleeping bag moving as Anita gave Jeff more presidential treatment. Juanita knew that she was trying to make it so that Jeff would never want to be without her. She too slipped down into the sleeping bag and gave Bill more presidential treatment. The men moaned softly in their sleep. They smiled and dreamed sweetly. Jeff dreamed that he was floating on a woman's silk handkerchief. He was naked in the dream and the silk was drifting gently across him in a warm breeze. Bill dreamed that he was floating in a large bowl of whipped cream. The sensuous cream pressed upon his entire body. It was smooth and soft. He felt like he was floating on air.

Jim woke up to the sounds of the birds chirping outside. The sparrows were mating and making a terrible racket. Robins were singing. It appeared that it would be hard to sleep in late. He got up and took a shower. Then he cooked up enough bacon and egg omelets for everyone. He also made his favorite buttered toast with a mixture of sugar and cinnamon on top. Finally when everything was ready, he went to the bedroom to wake the fishermen. The legs of the girls were sticking out of the sleeping bags, and their heads were making the bags move up and down in the middle. He smiled and went back to the galley. He decided that the men wouldn't mind cold breakfast. He certainly wasn't going to interrupt them now.

Finally in about 30 minutes, the men had started to feel more eager. Soon there was a gentle moaning duet coming from the bedroom. Jim could hear it and smiled to himself. He quietly ate his bacon before it got cold. He kept the rest simmering on the stove. Finally, when the moaning had subsided, he called to the love birds, "Breakfast is ready. Come and get it." The girls reluctantly pulled themselves off the men and quickly dressed. The men got dressed too. They all went to the kitchen and had breakfast.

Anita said, "I want to confess that Juanita and I took a shower with Jim Monday. We just washed him and rubbed up against him. No presidential treatment." Jeff said, "I don't mind. You'll be showering with lots of men this year." Bill said, "Yes, and Jim is like one of the family now. Just so that when we have a baby, I know that it is mine." Juanita said, "I promise. No going all the way with other men." Jeff said, "Why don't you both take off your tops? Jim might appreciate the view. Juanita said, "Are you sure it's all right." Bill said, "It's all right." Jim said, "I wouldn't complain." The girls took off their tops. Juanita said, "Jim will be seeing lots of us this winter. He might as well get used to us now." They all ate the food Jim had prepared for them. Juanita said, "I love this sweet cinnamon coated bread and butter. Where did you learn to make it?" Jim said, "My mother always made it for me when I was a child." She died when I was 52. I'm 60 now, so that would be eight years ago. She was 72 years old when she died. My father died six months later. They both died of heart attacks. My father was 85 when he died. It's a quick death. Much better than dying a slow painful death, like when you die of cancer."

Juanita said, "I shouldn't have gotten you talking about your mother. Death is such a terrible subject for breakfast conversation. But since we're on the subject, I will tell you that my father almost lost his life to sharks. He was taking some tourists fishing in a small boat. He slipped and fell into the sea. A shark took off his left leg before they got him back into the boat. He thought sure he was going to die. One of the tourists put a tourniquet on his stub of a leg and saved his life." Jim said, "That would be a terrible way to die. I don't want to be around sharks, ever!" Bill said, "I can do without sharks, too." Jeff said, "I would like to fish for some, but I would be real careful about slipping into the water."

Anita said, "Can't we talk about something else. I just ate." Jeff said, "Let's talk about just exactly what you intend to do with men in the shower at your massage parlor." Anita said, "We would let them undress us and then we would let them rub us all over with soap. Then we would rub them with soap. We would use some nonirritating soap so that we could use it to give a man a special message in the shower. Juanita and I would both work together on each man. That way he would feel controlled, and he would get more excited. If the shower didn't get him completely off, we would move him to a massage table. We would take turns massaging him just the right way, so that he would be completely satisfied. Do I have to spell it out more than that?" Jeff said, "No, I think I get the picture. How much will you charge for the shower and massage? Does everyone get the massage, even if they were made excited enough in the shower?" Anita said, "Everyone gets a shower and a massage. The charge would be $100. Jim thinks that is a reasonable price." Jim said, "The men here will be glad to pay that much. Most of the prostitutes in Fairbanks aren't as good looking as Juanita and Anita. They aren't as romantic either. No shower and no massage. If you want that much time from one of them, you would need to pay several hundred dollars. Also there aren't many prostitutes in Fairbanks. The law keeps them on the run. They won't bother a massage parlor, as long as the showering and nudity is kept secret. Nobody is going to watch all day to see what you are massaging on whom."

Jeff said, "How many customers would you expect in one day?" Anita said, "We could have 30 a day, if we worked 10 hours a day and spent 20 minutes on each one. That would be 10 minutes in the shower and 10 for the body massage. We could make $3,000 a day. Jim wants 20%, so he would get $600 a day. Juanita and I would make around $1,000 a day each. We would work six days a week, 26 days a month. In four months we should each have $100,000 after expenses." Jeff said, "That is a lot of money. We could afford to retire in Mexico on that much." Anita said, "And you should have some money from your divorce settlement too." Jeff said, "Yes, I should get a little over $100,000." Bill said, "I will only get about $40,000, but it should be enough. We won't need to worry about money."

Jim said, "I'll have $60,000 from the winter's work. I think I might retire in Mexico too. Loreto sounds like a nice place. My little house would only go for about $35,000. I would keep my boat. I might keep the house too and just stay in Mexico during the cold months. I think I would miss the fishing guide business. Maybe you girls could set me up with a nice young girl in Mexico to marry." Anita said, "For a man like you, with character and money; you could take your pick. There are plenty of attractive young women in Loreto." Jim said, "That sounds great. Seeing you girls has rekindled my interest in women. I would promise to keep my new wife away from the bears." He shook his head as he remembered the unfortunate end of his last wife. Jim looked at the beautiful small brown nipples on the girl's breasts. He said, "Yes, you girls are inspiring. On the cold nights here in Alaska a man needs a warm good looking woman to make him realize what life is all about. Too much playing cards and drinking whiskey with the guys, isn't good for a fellow. He needs a woman to help him want to succeed, and to keep him from getting lonely at night.

I want you and Juanita to find me a woman with your same mental attitude, Anita. She must want very much to give all the pleasure that she can to her man. Sure, I'm 60 years old, but if I have a woman around, I want her to give me what I want sexually." Anita said, "You mean the presidential treatment? Jim said, "What is the presidential treatment?" Anita said, "Do you remember when the President of the United States got in trouble with his female assistant?" Jim said, "Yes, I remember that." Anita said, "She bl-w the President. That is what you want, whenever you want it, right?" Jim said, "That would be wonderful. That's the kind of woman I want." Anita said, "We will find you a woman like that. Our women don't use that for bait just to hook a man. We stay the same after marriage. Many American women play tricks to get their men, and then change after marriage. They no longer feel like giving the presidential treatment. It is a big chore for them. And finally they will do it no more. Then they wonder why some young girl was able to steal their husband away so easily. They deserve what they get. Right?"

Jim said, "I wouldn't like a woman changing that way. I would feel tricked or taken for granted." Jeff said, "That's what my wife did. She got so I had to beg her for sex. There was never any presidential treatment." Bill said, "My wife gave me the presidential treatment. She was just loosing her enthusiasm. She always seemed tired and bored. I could tell that she wasn't excited with me like she used to be. I have to admit that it is more exciting for me to have a young woman, and I really like Juanita's brown skin. It looks healthy and attractive." Juanita said, "Thank you, Bill. I'm starting to think that possibly you actually will divorce your wife. I think you are still quite attached to her. I don't know what I can do about that. One day soon, you will have to make a final decision. I think I can make you happier than she can. You have to give her up." Bill said, "I will decide in the next couple months. I'm almost sure that I will leave her. I just want to be sure before I tell you for certain. I don't know how I will feel when I see her again." Juanita said, "I'm patient. I'll wait for you to make up your mind."

Jim said, "I think we might as well head back to Alakanuk. I'll untie the boat and start it up. Anita said, "Wait, Jim. I was thinking. Why should we go back now? How many towns are there between here and Fairbanks?" Jim said, "I'd say about 15 towns. Why do you ask?" Anita said, "We could start giving massage at the taverns. We could make a lot of money in 30 days. We could stay for two days in each town. That way word could get around. The second day would be pretty busy." Jim said, "I like your business sense. Will the men go for it?" Anita said, "Let's ask them." She went below and asked Jeff and Bill, "Would you mind if Juanita and I spend two days in each of 15 towns between here and Fairbanks giving massage. It would help advertise our new business in Fairbanks." Jeff said, "I don't mind. Bill and I will fish the river and shoot some more bears." Bill said, "I wouldn't mind getting a rifle and bear license myself. But what will our wives say about us staying here that long?" Jeff said, "It will only be two and a half weeks. I'll call and tell them about the bear hunting. They won't mind if we're having lots of fun. I'll promise them a trip to Florida." Bill said, "That sounds like a good plan. Call today."

Anita said, "I think we should go to the tavern and ask John to let us give massages in his bar. It will help his business too." Jim said, "I'll tie the boat back up." They all went back to the bar and talked to John. He said, "I like that idea. I'll call everyone I know. When will you start?" Anita said, "We'll need to buy some more body lotion." John said, "They have it at the trading post. When can you start?" Anita said, "We'll be ready by 12:00 o'clock noon today. We'll work here today and tomorrow. Then we'll move up river to the next town." John said, "I'll call them so they will be expecting you. You'll be booked solid I think." Anita said, "Thanks for the help John." She shook the big man's hand and caressed his thick red hair. She said, "Do you have a shower in this place?" John said, "Sure, I live in the back room." Anita said, "How would you like to be our first customer?" John said, "I'd be honored. Why do you want the shower?" Anita said, "We always shower with our customers first. They need to be clean for the massage. Juanita and I will shower naked with you. We hope to make you feel very good in the shower. We can make your pleasure continue after the shower if you give us a place to massage you." John said, "You can use my bed." Anita said, "We guarantee that you will be happy when we are done. We use lotion and massage on every part of your body." John said, "I'm looking forward to that."

The girls worked all day and through the evening at the bar. When they returned to the boat, they each had $1,200 and Jim had his $600. Bill and Jeff had been fishing from the boat, and caught several nice sized kings. Jeff was cooking one of them in the galley when the girls and Jim returned. Jeff said, "Did anyone give you any trouble?" Juanita said, "They were all quite nice. I never thought there were so many men who longed for the touch of a woman." Anita said, "They really made us feel appreciated. What town is next after tomorrow, Jim?" Jim said, "We go to St. Mary's next, and then Pitkas." Jeff said, "Bill and I called our wives. They were glad that we're having a good time. I told them we would be back in about four and a half weeks. I'll ship them each a bear skin rug."

Juanita said, "I thought of a way that we can make even more money. Most of the men did mention that they would like to go all the way with a pretty Mexican girl. I thought of a 19 year old prostitute from Loreto named Luisa Gonzalez. She is a little heavier than we are, but she has an attractive body. She does anything a man can think of. I think she would be popular on the river. She might get us arrested in Fairbanks, but we could take her up and down the river till November when we open the parlor in Fairbanks. The men would save up their money and pay a couple hundred for her. She would give us half the money for finding the customers for her." Jeff said, "That sounds logical. How much do you think it would make for us?" Juanita said, "I think that our half would be up to $200,000." Jeff said, "I'll arrange for her to get a telegram and a plane ticket to Anchorage. From there we'll have her flown to the next town up the river." Juanita said, "I know she'll want to come and help us. She likes her work, and she loves money. She'll always be a prostitute. No one man is enough for her."

Jim said, "I will get 20% of her income off the top, right." Anita said, "That is only fair. We'll all be staying in your boat." Jim said, "I'm in favor of it then. For that kind of money I'll sleep on the floor." Anita said, "You can sleep with us. We trust you. Besides, Luisa will keep you sexually satisfied for no charge. She is always longing for another man." Jim said, "I'll see to it that all the men have rubbers. We don't want to start some epidemic of V.D. along the river."

Bill said, "If you girls stay and work all summer, fall and winter; how much will you each make?" Anita said, "We should each have over $300,000 if we work 10 hour days and six days a week." Bill said, "That's plenty of money, but how can you girls take that many showers?" Anita said, "That is a good point. We may have to shorten the showers, or charge more for them." Bill said, "That sounds like a plan. After this year, there will be no more touching other men, right?" Juanita said, "At last you are starting to sound a little jealous. If you leave your wife, I will be loyal to you and share all my money with you." Bill said, "That sounds good to me. I can't wait till we are alone together in Loreto." Juanita said, "That time will come before you know it."

Anita said, "Jeff, you can send the airplane ticket to our motel in Loreto. Maria knows where Luisa lives. She will give her the ticket. I want to call Maria tomorrow and tell her we won't be back until April 1st. I'll tell Maria what to tell Luisa." Jeff said, "We can have the charter plane service pick Luisa up at the airport and fly her to the next town." Jim said, "Remember, St. Mary's is the next town. She can meet us at the town tavern. There's only one." Jeff said, "We'd better get some sleep, we have another big day ahead of us tomorrow. I have a fish simmering on the stove. We'd better eat and then get to bed." They all went to the galley and ate fresh salmon with bread and butter. There was cold beer to drink. They weren't in the mood for whiskey. They each had a couple beers and went to bed.

The girls worked at the tavern the next day, and Bill and Jeff continued fishing for kings and Arctic char. The girls returned to the boat at midnight and went straight to bed. They said they had eaten some hamburgers at the tavern. Everyone slept soundly.

Early the next morning, Jim steered the boat up stream to St. Mary's. Jeff woke up early and made breakfast for everyone in the galley. When he had the food ready he woke up the others. He enjoyed watching the girls get dressed. They both had wonderful slender brown bodies. He was starting to get in the mood for some loving with Anita. Bill also watched the girls dress. He was interested to do something other than just fishing. The girls had been too tired after their long day of work. He whispered in Juanita's ear that he was interested in some fun that morning. She said, "After breakfast, Anita and I have a nice surprise." They all went to breakfast and ate bacon and pancakes with maple syrup.

After eating Juanita said, "Jim bought dozens of rubbers for the men in the taverns to use. He gave us some for you guys. Now we can do whatever you want to do." Jeff said, "They aren't 100% effective you know." Juanita said, "Even if we do get pregnant, we will have plenty of money by the time we would be showing." Jeff said, "I would rather wait. I'm happy with what we are doing now." Bill said, "I agree. It's too much money to risk. In November we can come for a visit. Then it will be late enough that is won't matter." Juanita said, "That will give us something to look forward to." Anita said, "I can't believe you guys are so responsible. I can't stand any more showers right now. Just lay down in the bedroom. Juanita and Bill can have the galley." The couples parted company and the girls did their favorite things to the men. The girls were full of desire after seeing so many men that they couldn't give presidential treatment to. They got excited and breathed heavily as they made things more and more presidential.

The next day went much like the last day, except there were many more customers. The customers liked the idea of the new expensive prostitute from Mexico who would be with them in a couple weeks. Their eyes widened when they were told that she was beautiful and would do anything they could dream of. Juanita told one customer, "If she really likes the way you make love to her, she will ask you to bite her neck just hard enough to leave a hickey. She wears the hickey to honor you for your excellence in love making." The man said, "I will make her beg for several hickeys. She'll want more of me." Then he puffed out his chest and smiled. Juanita said, "Just remember to save your money. She's expensive."

Jeff and Bill spent the day bear hunting. Towards evening Bill got his first bear. It was another brown bear. They were close to town and down by the river when he shot it. Bill had bought his license there in Mountain Village. He bought his 30-06 Remington there too. It was a used one with a nice mint condition walnut stock. He shot it in the heart and it died instantly. Jeff said, "I'm impressed with your marksmanship. Where did you learn to shoot like that?" Bill said, "I grew up with a 22 caliber rifle in my hand. They aren't that different. The 30-06 just kicks harder." Jeff said, "That's for sure. It's about like a 12 gauge shotgun. We'd better have the owner of the trading post send someone to get this bear and tan it. We'll pay them and have them send it to your wife." Bill said, "No, I'll send it to the motel in Loreto. I'm going to get my divorce right away. I can't stand thinking about hiding Juanita from my wife any longer. I want to get everything over with as soon as possible." Jeff said, "I know what you mean. I think I'll call a lawyer tomorrow and have him start working up some divorce papers. You can use the same lawyer if you like." Bill said, "Yes, we can both talk to the lawyer tomorrow. That way we will be free to marry the girls in April." Jeff said, "Let's not rush into the marriage part. They are treating us royally now. Let's not spoil it. I'm going to make Anita wait a year or two." Bill said, "You may be right. Possibly all women stop trying as hard after they're married. I'll wait awhile too."

They walked to the trading post and told the owner what they wanted. His name was Phil. He was a strong looking man with a stocky build. He looked like he was about 40 years old. Phil had red hair and a beard with moustache. He said, "I'll have my brother Tim, tan that bear for you. It will be about a month before it's ready to ship. The shipping will be $100 and the tanning will be $75." Bill paid him the money and said to Jeff, "That about cleans me out." Jeff said, "You can ask Juanita for some more money. She will be glad to give you more." Bill said, "I feel funny about asking her for money. We aren't married yet." Jeff said, "She's been telling everyone you are engaged to her. Why don't you tell her that you're talking to a lawyer tomorrow and that you want her to promise to marry you in a year or two?" Bill said, "I think I'll do that, but I still don't want to ask her to give me money." Jeff said, "Here's $100 to last you till she gives you some more. I know she is generous. She will make sure you have enough money." He handed the $100 to Bill. Bill said, "Thanks for the money. I'll make sure you get it back." Jeff said, "I'll pay the lawyer for you too. He won't start any paper work until he gets paid. I can use my credit card over the phone." Bill said, "I appreciate it. I think I'll just wait for my wife to get the papers in the mail. I can't think how to bring up the topic of divorce with her." Jeff said, "I know what you mean. It will be difficult. I'm going to tell my wife as soon as I get home. Then I'll get a cottage by Lake Wawasee so that I can fish every day until the divorce comes through." Bill said, "If you don't mind, I might join you. We could split the rent." Jeff said, "That sounds fine. We can fish for bluegill together. We can talk to the girls in the mornings on the cell phone. They will be glad to hear that we are in a place of our own."

Phil had been listening to all this. He said, "So you're trading the old models in." Jeff said, "We were fishing in Loreto, Mexico and met two 19 year old beautiful young women who were our fishing guides. One thing led to another. Now they are up here getting rich giving massages." Phil said, "Yes, I heard that they shower with the men too. They must be making a lot of money, but aren't you two jealous?" Jeff said, "We need the money. The girls have a manager named Jim, who makes sure that the men don't try to go too far. We can trust the girls. They just want to make money quick so we can all retire comfortably." Phil said,

"That sounds good. Where will you live?" Jeff said, "In April they will finish four months of work in Fairbanks. After that, we will live with them in Loreto, Mexico. We plan on doing plenty of travel to various fishing destinations around the world." Phil said, "Sounds wonderful. I'm going over to the tavern this evening myself and shower with your women. I here they are quite beautiful and slender." Bill said, "They are attractive. I hope you enjoy it. There isn't that much fun to be had in many places along the river." Phil said, "I think you're right. I'm looking forward to that new girl you're bringing up in a couple weeks. Luisa sounds like a lot of fun." Jeff said, "Word travels fast in this town." Phil said, "Jim told everyone at the café this morning. He said we can do anything we want with her, as long as we don't hurt her. He said she likes it too. And she is friendly and has a sense of humor." Jeff said, "Sounds like you can't go wrong. We're going to the restaurant. Have you had lunch?" Phil said, "I would like to come along. I can close the store for an hour. I wonder what the special is today."

They left the store and walked to the restaurant. It was just across from the tavern. It was just a small log cabin with a few small windows. They went in and sat down and ordered coffee. The owner had no waitress. He waited on them himself. He said, "The special is roast beef on bread with mashed potatoes and gravy." All the men ordered the special. Phil said, "This is Bob, the owner of the restaurant. Bob, this is Jeff and Bill. They are the fiancées of the girls who are showering and massaging at the tavern." Bob said, "I heard they are incredibly nice to look at. Don't you guys get jealous about them giving massages to the men?" Jeff said, "As long as they don't do more than that, we can live with it. We need the money. We all want to retire next April. There is a girl named Luisa who is coming up from Mexico to do the more intense sexual things with the men." Bob said, "I heard about her this morning. We will be looking forward to her. I hope she stays after your girls retire." Jeff said, "Jim may continue to work with her. We haven't discussed that yet. It sounds like a possibility though."

Bob left to serve up their food. He brought it out in just a few minutes. He gave them their food and said, "I might as well close early. Everyone is over at the tavern waiting for their shower and massage." Phil said, "I might as well close early too. They won't be back for a couple weeks. This town has never had this much excitement. I want to make sure that I don't get left out." They all ate their food and paid Bob. Jeff and Bill went to the boat and fished for awhile. Bill said, "Now that I'm more certain that I want to marry Juanita, I'm starting to get a little jealous." Jeff said, "We just need to stay busy. We can spend some quality time with the girls in the mornings. We should have a campfire tomorrow morning along the river bank. We could cook breakfast on the open fire. That reminds me. We need to call Alakanuk and have someone take our tent down and store it." Bill said, "Yes, I forgot all about the tent and stove. I think when we get to St. Mary's, we should rent a room for the four of us. The boat is too crowed for all of us to live on constantly. Luisa could stay with Jim on the boat, or they could each stay where ever they want to in town." Jeff said, "The boat is starting to feel a little cramped. I would like to rent a nice place with a big shower. The one in the boat is fun, but it would be fun to try something a little bigger." Bill said, "I like that idea. A nice wide bed would be nice too. We may have to rent two places. Most places don't have two big beds." Jeff said, "You're right, but it is fun watching both girls dress in the morning. Maybe we should stay on the boat a little longer." Bill said, "Right, why mess with a good thing? It saves us lots of money."

Jeff said, "We do need some privacy to propose to the girls. We should do it the same day, so one doesn't get jealous." Bill said, "Why not tomorrow in St. Mary's. We'll be meeting Luisa there. We could have the girls take Saturday off so that we could get to know Luisa, and later we could propose to the girls." Bill said, "That sounds like a good plan. We can tell them that divorces take a long time, and we will need to wait two years to actually marry them." Jeff said, "We need to marry them so that we will be entitled to half of all their money." Bill said, "I never thought of that. Without Juanita's money, I would be fairly poor if I divorce my wife. We should marry them as soon as the divorces go through then." Jeff said, "Yes, and we need to have them get wills with us as the beneficiaries. You can't be too careful. What if something would happen to them?" Bill said, "I would only have the $40,000 from the divorce. I could get by in Mexico, but I wouldn't be able to see the world or travel like I could with the kind of money Juanita is making." Jeff said, "Once they have their wills finished, we won't need to worry so much. There are always more young girls in Mexico. I'm afraid the money will change the girls and they will start treating us like my wife does, and make us beg for sex all the time." Bill said, "You may be right. Something sure went wrong with your wife's sexual attitude. My wife's only problem was getting old. She still is fairly eager to please sexually." Jeff said, "Maybe you should stay with your wife. She hasn't done anything to deserve being divorced." Bill said, "But I get more turned on by a young girl like Juanita." Jeff said, "The more I think about how things are, the less I trust the girls. I think they really enjoy all the attention from all these men. They won't be happy with just us. Don't repeat this, but if we didn't like them so much they would appear to be common whores. They wallow all over those men in the showers and then give them massages in intimate places. Those weren't our ideas. The girls wanted to do those things. I don't think they will be loyal to us. I say take as much of their money as we can and then get some unspoiled young girls that are more likely to be loyal. Then the money will be ours and it would tend to inspire loyalty in young girls." Bill said, "I never thought you were this cold and calculating." Jeff said, "Years of begging for sex makes you this way. If you don't control women they control you. That's what life is all about. Who controls whom?"

Bill said, "What are you saying we should do then, exactly?" Jeff said, "We should tell the girls we are divorcing our wives and marrying them. You can stay married to your wife if you want to. If something happens to the girls we will be wealthy. If nothing happens to them, we can still have fun for quite awhile with them.

If they develop bad attitudes we can divorce them and take half their money." Bill said, "That's quite a plan. How long have you been thinking about this?" Jeff said, "Ever since they wanted to do these showers and massages for men along the river. That's when I realized that they haven't changed any since they met us. They are still glorified whores, just like they were on the charter boat in Mexico, giving the presidential treatment to everyone who would give them a tip." Bill said, "I'm starting to understand your rather cold way of looking at them. I thought you were in love. You sure fooled me. I'm sure that you have the girls fooled." Jeff said, "I am in love. I'm in love with every girl who makes me feel good and isn't into a power trip. I won't be putting up with second rate sex anymore. Life is too short. I'm getting older." Bill said, "I'm getting older too. I like your plan for getting money, and I think I'll stay with my wife. If she finds out about the girls, I'll give up Juanita and go back to Sandy." Jeff said, "That's probably for the best. Your wife tries to please. She can't help it that she's getting older. At least she is loyal." Bill said, "You better call your lawyer today and ask him not to start my divorce papers. Tell him that I changed my mind." Jeff said, "Sure. Let's go into town now and call him."

They walked into town and used the pay phone in front of the post office. Jeff said, "This way no one will hear that you aren't getting a divorce from your wife. It's not too likely that anyone would tell the girls, but we can't be too careful." Bill said, "I agree. Let's be careful." Jeff talked to the lawyer briefly and explained what he wanted. Then the men walked around the town. It was only five blocks long. It didn't take long to get from one end of town to the other. Most of the buildings were small log cabins with tin roofs. They walked through town and then a little ways out into the woods. Jeff said, "Once the girls have made enough money, we should take them on some trips into the wilds. They like adventure. I'd like to see the Endicott Mountains near the Gates of the Arctic National Park and Preserve. Jim's been telling me about that area. He says it's beautiful there. We could fly to Barrow. It is the town that is furthest north in Alaska. It's in the National Petroleum Preserve." Bill said, "That all sounds fine to me." Jeff said, "The girls like excitement so much, we'll give it to them."

They walked a little farther into the woods until they saw a grizzly bear and her cub. Jeff said, "I wouldn't want to get too close to a grizzly. They have a reputation for attacking humans sometimes, especially when they have cubs with them." Jeff turned slowly and walked back towards town. Bill stayed close to him. They both looked frequently over their shoulders, to make sure the bears weren't following them. Jeff said, "Let's get our guns and do some target shooting." Bill said, "Good idea. I think being a good shot in this part of the country could save a person's life." They walked back to the boat and got their guns. They threw apples out into the river and practiced shooting them. They didn't use too many, because apples were expensive on the river. They knew that eventually the apples would end up along the shore and the bears would eat them. Jeff shot the first apple. He said, "I hit that one right in the middle. Did you see it explode?" Bill said, "Let me try." He fired, and the apple shot up into the air. He said, "I must have been just a little under it." Jeff said, "Go ahead and try another one." Bill aimed a little longer than the last time. Finally he squeezed off a shot. The apple shattered. He said, "I got that one." He tried several more, until he felt confident of his abilities. Jeff tried a couple more shots and was successful every time.

Bill said, "Let's drink a couple more beers and then go back to town we could call St. Mary's and rent a couple rooms. We can get John, the tavern owner, to tell us where would be a good place to rent." Jeff said, "Sounds good to me. Let's go." They put their guns away and headed for the tavern. Bill said, "Before you explained your plan to me, I would have been too jealous to go in the tavern where the girls are doing those things with other men. Now, I'm learning to be more detached and calculating. Like you." Jeff said, "You have to be that way. If you get too attached to a woman, she'll take advantage of you. It allows them to control you." Bill said, "I don't want that. I like being in control." Jeff said, "That's the spirit!"

They came to the tavern and walked in. John was at the bar as usual. Bill said, "John, where would be a couple of good places to rent in St. Mary's?" John said, "If you want to have a woman with you, you'll want to stay at Steve's cabins along the river. They are made for tourists. Each one has a king sized bed and nice deluxe shower with unlimited hot water. He provides firewood for the fireplaces and stoves. I think they are the only places in St. Mary's that are set up that nice." Bill said, "That sounds exactly like what we want. Do you have the phone number?" John said, "I keep it right here on the wall." John thought, "They are nice cabins, and I'll appreciate the $5.00 commission that Steve gives me on each customer that I send to him."

Jeff said, "Could I get a cheeseburger and some fries?" John said, "The grill is open. I can get you whatever you want. What about you, Bill?" Bill said, "I'll have the same thing, with catsup and relish." Jeff said, "I'll take catsup and relish too, and a Miller High Life." Bill said, "I'll take a whiskey and coke." John said, "Coming right up." While they waited for their food, Jeff and Bill watched as different men went into John's rooms in the back of the tavern. Jeff said, "As I watch those men going back there, I try to only think about the money." Bill said, "I know what you're going to say. You can't help but feel a little jealous." Jeff said, "That's right. Even though I'm not looking at Anita as a potential lifetime partner, I feel jealous. I guess it must be an instinct. I think that after the stay at St. Mary's that I'll go home for awhile. I'll feel better about the girls when they have all that money and can stop being with other men." Bill said, "I'll come with you. I don't want my wife wondering why we're staying here so long." Jeff said, "That's a good point. I'll call the charter plane service and have them pick us up at St. Mary's on Monday morning at 12:00 noon. We can have a nice weekend with the girls and meet Luisa. She will help to make us rich." Bill said, "I wonder what she looks like." Jeff said, "So far, every girl that we've met from Loreto has been good looking." Bill said, "I know." Jeff said, "We'd probably better not try her out. It could jeopardize the whole operation. We need to keep the girls thinking that we are loyal to them." Bill said, "I think that I can resist her. I don't like rubbers, and I'd never try a girl like that without one." Jeff said, "I don't mind rubbers all that much, but I like lots of money. I'm not going to let a little horniness ruin everything."

The food came, and Jeff and Bill ate it slowly as they continued to watch the men going into the back rooms. When the men came out, they were always happy and bragging to the other men about how much fun they had in the shower. Jeff and Bill finished their food and went back to the boat. They sat in the galley and drank whiskey while they played poker for dimes. Jeff said, "Once the girls are done working in April, we need to get them to put us in their wills. We can marry them if they insist on it as a condition before they'll put us in their wills. No one will know that you haven't divorced your wife." Bill said, "You aren't planning on arranging an accident for them are you?" Jeff said, "Not exactly. I just want to live dangerously with them. If something bad happens to them we win. If nothing bad happens, we win too. It's a win win situation. We can't lose." Bill said, "I guess I understand." Jeff said, "As long as we have no plan to do anything bad, we can't get into any trouble for it. Right?" Bill said, "That sounds logical." Jeff said, "The less you know the better. I just want to live dangerously for a year or two, or however long it takes. That way we won't get bored and neither will the girls." Jeff said, "Sounds fun. Just so we don't get hurt. What if one of the girls just gets badly hurt?" Jeff said, "When you get hurt badly in the mountains of Alaska, the odds are that the cold will finish you off. Now let's not talk about it anymore. We don't want premeditation in case of a court inquiry."

Jeff and Bill continued playing cards until past midnight when Jim and the girls returned to the boat. Anita said, "I made $4,800 dollars today. We each pleased a customer every 10 minutes for 10 hours. I'm pretty tired." Juanita said, "I'm tired too, but we could play a little cards before going to bed." They all sat in the galley and played poker. Jim said, "The men all knew that it was our last day there for a couple weeks. We had to run them through faster than usual." Jeff said, "Bill and I would like the girls to take Saturday and Sunday off to be with us. We are going back to Indiana at noon on Monday." Juanita said, "Why are you leaving so soon?" Jeff said, "We have done all the fishing we want to do here for now. We want to get our finances arranged a little differently before our wives hear about the divorces." Juanita said, "That sounds good. When will we get married?" Jeff said, "Bill and I were discussing that. We don't know how long the divorces will take. We can start acting like we are married now. Bill and I will change our wills so that if anything happens to us you and Anita will get our money. That's part of what love is all about." Juanita said, "I'll get a will right away. Bill will receive my money if I die." Anita said, "I'll get a will too. We can do it as soon as we get to Fairbanks."

Jeff said, "You girls are very mature for your ages. You want to see us protected in case you die. That is touching." Juanita said, "And you also are providing for me in case you die. It is like we are married already. Jeff said, "In April, when both of you are done working, Bill and I would like to take both of you to the Endicott Mountains. Juanita said, "Where are they?" Jeff said, "They are north of here quite a ways. It will be cold, but we can dress warm and take a good tent with us." Anita said, "That sounds exciting. It will be something we can tell our children about." Juanita said, "That is just the kind of excitement I was hoping for. I'm tired of the heat in Mexico. It will be fun to see what the far North Country is like. I love tents. They are so cozy." Anita said, "I like tents too. They are romantic." Anita slid a rubber across the table to Jeff and said, "I could use one more shower tonight. Are you ready?" Jeff said, "That sounds good to me. The two went to the bedroom and stripped. They came back through the kitchen with towels wrapped around them and went into the shower. Bill, Juanita and Jim continued playing poker. They laughed every time they started to hear thumping sounds on the side of the shower. Juanita said, "Jeff must have her up against the wall." Jim said, "That's what it sounds like to me." After about an hour, the couple left the shower and went to bed.

Bill and Juanita took their turn in the shower. He loved looking at her naked brown body under the steaming water. He wished that he wasn't so old. He sensed that what Jeff had said about the girls was probably true. They would never be loyal to an older man who wasn't rich. "Even a rich man would have trouble keeping a young girl's loyalty if he was a lot older," thought Bill. Finally he tried to put such thoughts aside and concentrated on the nice things that Juanita was doing to him. He pushed her gently to her knees. She was starting to understand that he had a strong need for lots of presidential treatment. After about an hour Juanita managed to get Bill to finish. He was learning to like her more every time she did that. "I will protect her," he thought. He wanted her around. There might not be any others like her. Just so she didn't push too hard for marriage. That could ruin the thrill of it. When they left the shower, they saw that Jim had fallen asleep on the bench seat of the galley table. They quietly slipped past him and went to the bedroom, where they crawled into their sleeping bag and went to sleep.

Early the next morning Jim untied the boat and headed it up stream towards St. Mary's. It was only about 20 miles away. They made the trip in only two hours. Jim tied the boat to the main pier, and hooked up the electricity. He cooked up a large stack of pancakes and then awakened everyone. They all got dressed and went to the galley for breakfast. Jeff said, "I reserved a couple cabins for Bill and me to take the girls to. That means that you can have the boat, Jim. Jim said, "It will be nice to stretch out on the bed tonight." Juanita said, "Luisa should be here by noon today. We said we would meet her at the town's tavern. Why don't we look the place over? We can schedule ourselves to work there Monday and Tuesday." Jim said, "That sounds like a good idea." They all walked to the tavern. It was right on the water front. They would be able to see Luisa's plane land from there. The Tavern was full of men who had heard that girls were coming to the place. They all wanted to buy the girls drinks. The girls would only drink cokes, since it was only 9:00 o'clock in the morning.

The tavern's owner, Steve, was about 45 years old with long black hair and a moustache. He was thin and about six feet tall. When he brought the cokes to the girls, he said, "You and these men must be the people who rented the cabins by the river for two days. Who do I talk to about payment?" Juanita said, "I'll pay. How much is it?" Steve said, "Those are deluxe cabins. Each one is $40 per night." Juanita said, "Here's a hundred." Steve brought her the change and said, "The men are looking forward to showers and massages. They are also eager to see Luisa. Did I understand Jeff right on the phone when he said that she does anything the men want to do?" Juanita said, "Luisa will be happy to do anything that isn't painful. She likes variety." Steve smiled and said, "She'll be quite popular here. There aren't any women like that here now." Jeff said, "The girls won't start working till Monday at 2:00 in the afternoon." Jim said, "I'm their manager. I'll be here with them to time the customers and charge them accordingly." Steve said, "I'm glad to meet you." He shook Jim's hand. Steve said, "I won't charge for the use of my shower and beds if Luisa will do what I ask her to do for 30 minutes each day." Juanita said, "I'm sure that Luisa will find that to her liking. She likes thin men especially well. And your black moustache is attractive too." Steve smiled and said, "Thank you. What's your name?" Juanita introduced herself and the others.

Jim said, "We are expecting Luisa to arrive at noon. We told her that we would meet her here." Steve said, "I'll give all of you a fifty percent discount on food and drink while you are here. It is the least I can do for such wonderful guests." Jim said, "That's very generous of you. I'd like a tall glass of cold milk." Steve said, "Coming right up. Anyone else?" They all said that they would take milk. When Steve returned with the milk, Jim said, "I think we could all use some bacon, well done. I made pancakes this morning, but I didn't take time to cook bacon." Steve said, "No problem." He left for 10 minutes and returned with a stack of plates and the one on top was heaped up with steaming crisp bacon." He passed out the plates and then divided up the bacon. Everyone dug in and ate the bacon while it was still hot.

They all sat around and talked to Steve and his customers until they saw Luisa's plane land on the river. They all went down to the dock to meet her. Luisa climbed out of the plane and shook everyone's hand. They all introduced themselves. She had long black hair and a wonderful figure. She wore low cut faded jeans that allowed a good view of her flat and attractive tummy. Luisa's face was that of a movie star. She was as attractive as Anita or Juanita. The men took her big suitcases into the boat. Then they went with Luisa to the tavern. Luisa said, "It was a long trip. It's good to be here, finally." Jim said, "It's good to have you here. I'll be your manager. We don't start work till Monday. Anita and Juanita want to spend some time with Jeff and Bill before they return to Indiana." Luisa said, "It's too bad that you have to leave. We can get to know each other this weekend at least." Jeff said, "I'm looking forward to that. Bill and I are staying with Anita and Juanita at two cabins by the river. You can come see us anytime." Luisa said, "That sounds wonderful. Where will I stay?" Jim said, "You can stay on the boat with me, or you can rent a place in town." Luisa said, "I'll stay on the boat. I've never slept on a big boat before. It will be fun." Jim said, "We should all have a walk around town. It will be good for business if people see how nice all you girls look. Then I'll show you the boat, Luisa." Luisa said, "I'm looking forward to that."

They walked slowly around the small town. There were many tall pine trees surrounding the town. The landscape was fairly flat, with occasional small hills in the distance. They looked at all the log buildings and talking to the friendly people. It wasn't often that strangers came to St. Mary's. Everyone wanted to know who the girls were. Most of them had heard Steve say that girls would be arriving. The men were obviously interested in the girls and shook their hands warmly. One middle aged man named Evertt came out of his house when he saw them walking by. He said, "I'll be at the tavern every evening. I'll see all of you there." He waved and then turned and went to his porch where he sat on a chair and watched them move on down the road. Several other men came out of their houses and said hello. They were obviously delighted to see the girls. One man, named Rueben, said, "I haven't seen women as nice looking as you three, for my entire life. Whatever you're selling at the tavern; I want some!"

The girls liked the interest shown by the men of St. Mary's, but it was starting to get close to 12:00 o'clock noon. Luisa said, "I could use something to eat. I didn't get anything on the plane." Jim said, "We can eat again at the tavern. Steve gives us half off on food and drink." Luisa said, "That sounds good to me." The others all agreed. They walked at a faster pace back to the tavern. Steve was having a special on rainbow trout. Jeff asked, "Where do the rainbow trout come from?" Steve said, "The locals catch them right out of the river with night crawlers." Jeff said, "Jim, why didn't you tell us about the rainbow trout?" Jim said, "I usually figure that visitors like the bigger fish. The rainbow are good to eat. They just run a little smaller on the average. You can fish for them if you like. They are usually swimming along the bottom of the river. They like salmon eggs when they are in season, but it's not quite time for that yet." Jeff said, "I know what Bill and I will fish for today. When is the best time to catch them?" Jim said, "They'll bite all day, but the best time is in the morning and late evening." Jeff said, "We'll start at around 6:00 o'clock then. That should give us plenty of time to fish. Where do we get the night crawlers?" Jim said, "The trading post should have some. We can go there after we eat." Jim told Steve, "I'll have the trout special with french fries and a Jack Daniels and coke." Jeff said, "I'll take the same." Bill said, "I think I'll have a cheeseburger. We will be eating our own trout this evening." Jeff said, "I forgot about that. Change mine to a cheeseburger." Juanita said, "I'll take a cheeseburger and Jack Daniels with coke." Anita said, "I'll have the same." Luisa said, "I'll have a bacon lettuce and tomato sandwich, please, on white toast."

Steve poured the drinks right away, and then went to the kitchen to prepare the food. He returned in about 20 minutes with all the things they had ordered. As they ate Jeff told Jim, "In the spring, I would like to take Bill, Juanita and Anita to the Endicott Mountains. What do you think?" Jim said, "It will be cold and windy that time of year. There would be more sun light and less frigid cold in August." Jeff said, "I wanted us to celebrate as soon as the girls were done working, in April. Jeff said, "Since you aren't experienced with the Arctic cold and mountains, I would recommend that you go to the Kaiyuh Mountains. They are right along the Yukon River. Then if you really like the mountains, you could go to the Endicott Mountains in August." Jeff said, "That sounds like a good plan.

I would like to shoot a polar bear. Are they protected?" Jim said, "I'll have to check at the trading post. I've never had anyone ask about shooting one." Bill said, "I would like to take one home, too." Juanita said, "Yes, home to the wife you are so loyal to." Bill said, "Let's not argue about that. We are going to spend some good time together. That's what is important." Juanita said, "I'm sorry Bill. I just wish you weren't leaving Monday." Bill said, "It's too bad that I need to go. I can call every day." Juanita said, "When will you visit Fairbanks?" Bill said, "I could probably come out in November before the weather gets too bad. My budget doesn't allow for too much travel. Jeff has a lot more money than I have." Juanita said, "I will pay your expenses. It won't cost you a thing. You can tell your wife that Jeff is paying for it." Bill said, "If you think that's a good idea, I'll do it. Jeff, should we come back in November?" Jeff said, "I can come then. We could use bear hunting as an excuse to come back."

They finished their meals and went down to the pier to show Luisa the boat. The sun was out and the river glistened with light. Pine trees lined the banks of the river and spread out for as far as the eye could see. Jim showed Luisa the boat's galley and shower. Then he showed her the bedroom. Luisa said, "I think I will like staying with you here, Jim. You are a handsome man, and it will be fun being alone with you here." She squeezed his hand and gave him a kiss on the lips. Jim said, "I think you are a fine woman. It will be fun to spent time with you here on the boat." Luisa said, "Jeff, could you go to the trading post without Jim? I'd like to talk with him alone for awhile about our business relationship." Jeff said, "Sure, the rest of us will all go to the trading post and find out about polar bear hunting." Jeff, Bill, Juanita and Anita went back into town and left Jim and Luisa alone together on the boat.

Jim sat at the galley table with Luisa beside him. She said, "How much do I pay you for being my manager?" Jim said, "The girls are giving me 20% or their gross earnings. That will be fine." Luisa said, "I have to give the girls 50% of my earnings. That only leaves 30% for me." Jim said, "Since you are paying the girls that much, I will pay for your food and lodging if you stay with me like you are my wife. It will be cheaper that way." Luisa said, "Like your wife. I like that. I would like for people to see me living with such a fine man. You've got a deal. Will I be having sex with you?" Jim said, "That is up to you. I don't want to assume that. I like you though. It would be fine with me. It isn't required." Luisa said, "I had a long flight from Mexico. I would like to take a shower. You can join me." Jim said, "I'd be glad to." They went to the bedroom took off most of their clothes. Jim politely helped Luisa get her bra off. He looked at her nice full breasts and smiled. He said, "You will feel nice and warm on cool nights." Luisa said, "Yes, feel them." She shoved her warm breasts up tight against his bare chest and gave him a long hug. Then she let him watch as she slowly slipped off her pants and panties. Her slender firm hips were tempting to him. He guided her to the shower and they got in.

Luisa scrubbed herself good in the steamy hot shower. She said, "It's nice and cozy in here. I like the steam." Jim said, "Yes, the water is nice and hot." Luisa soaped up Jim and washed him thoroughly. She said, "How do you feel about me doing so much with the men?" Jim said, "I look at it like dating. You are dating lots of men. It's just that they give you money. After a year you will have enough money that you can quit working if you want." Luisa said, "I'm glad you see it that way. My last manager didn't respect me. He was mean to me. That's why I was so eager to come here." Luisa whispered in Jim's ear, "Is it good for us to do some things now, here in the shower?" Jim said, "Whatever you want is fine with me." Luisa said, "Good." She slid down to

her knees and made Jim feel excellent. He couldn't help but
finish quickly, but Luisa kept on. They tried many unique
positions that Luisa was familiar with. The last one had Luisa's
legs wrapped around Jim.

Slowly, Luisa let her feet come back down to the floor. Jim
said, "You are great, Luisa. We can do this often." Luisa said,
"Yes, this is the kind of showering that I like. We will stay very
clean together." Luisa washed Jim off again and slid back onto
her knees. Jim said, "Wouldn't you be more comfortable in the
bed?" She said, "That will be nice too." Then she went back to
work. Jim couldn't believe his good fortune to find such a wonderful
woman. Finally, about an hour later then went to the bedroom
and resumed their activities.

At the trading post Jeff was talking with Howard Simons, the
owner. Jeff said, "Is it legal to kill polar bears?" Howard was a
tall thin man with brown hair and moustache. He said, "They are
protected most of the time. When the Department of Natural
Resources sees there are too many of them, they will allow a
limited hunt. You need to apply and get on a waiting list." Jeff
said, "That sounds like too much trouble. I'll just stick with
shooting brown bears. There seem to be plenty of them." Howard
said, "There are a lot of them. You can shoot one down by the
river almost any day of the week." Jeff said, "Are there wolves
around here?" Howard said, "There are plenty of wolves. You
don't want to hunt them though." Jeff said, "Why not?" Howard
said, "They travel in packs. They might get you instead of you
getting them." Jeff said, "That doesn't sound too good. I'll just
stick to brown bears." Bill asked, "How many brown bears can a
person kill?" Howard said, "Most people only want one per year.
They are expensive to tan and ship. If you have plenty of money
you can kill two per year." Bill said, "I already got one. I think
that will be enough this year." Jeff said, "I haven't decided yet.
One may be enough for me too. We'll be returning in November.
Bill will want to shoot one then and send it home, right Bill." Bill
said, "Yes, that's the official reason for my trip up here." Juanita
said, "But you are really coming to see me, right?" Bill said,

"You know that's the reason, Juanita. I just need a reason that will convince my wife." Jeff said, "Don't argue, you two." Juanita said, "I just wish he would decide who he wants most." Bill said, "We can go back to the boat and discuss this, Juanita."

They walked back to the boat. Jeff and Anita stayed and looked around the trading post some more. When Bill and Juanita got on the boat, they heard Luisa and Jim laughing and having a good time in the bedroom. They decided to go to the tavern. When they arrived, Steve was standing at the bar. Bill said, "Where is our cabin, Steve?" He said, "It's just east of here, by the river. Here's the key. Yours is the first log cabin that you come to." He handed Bill the key. Bill said, "I'd like a bottle of Jack Daniels and a six of coke, plus a bag of ice." Steve said, "I'll have my helper bring the stuff down. You can go on down there, if you like." Juanita and Bill went to the cabin and built a fire in the fireplace. It was about 4:00 o'clock. They lay on the bear skin rug in front of the fireplace. There was a knock on the door. It was the man with the supplies. Bill thanked him and said, "Have Steve put this on my bill, will you?" The old man said, "I sure will." He walked away and Bill closed the door. He poured a couple drinks and sat back down with Juanita. They drank in silence. Bill brought the whiskey bottle, cokes and ice over by the rug, just far enough from the fire so the ice wouldn't melt. He and Juanita had several more drinks. Finally Juanita said, "I don't mean to push too much, Bill. It's just that I'm falling in love with you. I can't understand why you won't leave your wife." Bill said, "I've been with her for a long time. She doesn't do anything wrong. I can't stand the thought of hurting her that much. She can't help it she is older than you. I like both of you. You turn me on more, because you are so young."

Juanita said, "I'm only doing this work with the men to get money so that we can retire comfortably. I'm not a whore. I just need money quickly. I will be loyal to you." Bill said, "I know you would be loyal. I just can't hurt my wife. I hope you will just give me time to be with you more. We can have fun during my visits to Loreto to do the maintenance work." Juanita said, "I will try to be patient, but you can't have both of us forever. Someday you will need to decide which of us you want." Bill said, "I will decide in two years. By then I will know." Juanita said, "Two years! That's a long time!" Bill said, "I know it seems like a long time. I need time to adjust. Maybe when you put me in your will, I will feel more like we are a couple. Right now, you have lots of money and I am poor." Juanita said, "If the money is keeping us apart, I will make out a will tonight. Let's get some paper and a pen." Bill went to the desk by one of the windows. There was paper and pen inside. Juanita said, "What shall I say?" Bill said, "You write it in your handwriting. I will tell you what to say." Juanita took the pen and started writing as Bill dictated. "I, Juanita Rojas, being of sound mind leave my money to my friend Bill Ellis. This is the 23rd day of April, 2003. This is my only will and testimony." Bill said, "Now all you have to do is sign this will in front of a witness. We could use Steve as the witness. Let's go over there now. That way we can put this behind us."

They went back to the tavern and Steve witnessed the signing of the will. Steve said, "I have a large safe. I could keep the will there for you, Juanita." Juanita said, "That sounds like a good idea." She gave the will to Steve. Steve said, "You must think a lot of Bill." Juanita said, "I will be marrying him in two years from now." Steve said, "Well that's good to hear. Hope you enjoy the cabin." The couple went back to the cabin. Bill poured a couple more drinks. Juanita started to take off her clothes. Bill said, "It isn't dark yet, Juanita." Juanita said, "I want you to see what you will be missing when you leave." She lay totally naked on her side on top of the bear rug. Bill watched her for a long time. Her brown shapely body was indeed tempting. The fire light flickered off her upturned breasts. Her small nipples were calling his lips to them. Her legs were so long and slender. Her firm shapely hips were perfect in every way. Bill thought to himself. "I could just never return to Indiana. But I can't marry Juanita if I don't divorce my wife. I could sign the papers and fax them to the lawyer. If I just didn't have to look her in the face and say that I'm divorcing her."

Juanita came over to Bill and took his clothes off him. She pulled him down onto the rug with her. She said, "I know that you don't like rubbers, Bill. I think that you like the presidential treatment the best of all. I want to make you very happy. She slid her face down along his chest to his waist and started licking his navel. Then she slowly licked her way down to what she really wanted. She held her hair back so that he could clearly watch as she gave him more and more of what he really wanted. She continued till the fire burned low and it got cold. She quickly put some more logs on the fire and went back to work on Bill. He longed to be with her always. His wife never did it for this long or this deeply. She didn't understand how much he liked it. Juanita was starting to win the battle for Bill's affections.

Anita and Jeff arrived at their cabin. Jeff started a fire. Anita put a case of cold Miller Lite in the refrigerator. They too lay on the bear rug that was in front of the fire. Anita had plenty of rubbers. She stripped and let Jeff look at her in the fire light. Jeff stripped too and started making out with Anita. She gave him plenty of the presidential treatment. Finally she put the rubber on him and let him do whatever he wanted to do. She was eager to cooperate. She drank some beer and then started some more presidential treatment. Jeff loved it, and let her do it as long as she wanted. She wanted it for a long long time. Finally, they tried some more positions and sat in front of the fire naked. They drank beer till late. Jeff had Anita made out a will that night. He said they would feel more like a couple that way. Anita was happy to do it.

Back on the boat, Jim and Luisa were just finishing with their fun in the bed. They were hungry and got up to cook some late night bacon and eggs. Luisa said, "If you want me to give up other men and marry you, I will." Jim said, "You came to work for Anita and Juanita. I hate to take you away from them. Why don't you just do a couple months on the river with them and then we'll get someone else for the Fairbanks work. I would like to be your only man. I just don't want you to have to live in my old house forever. We need to move to the tropics. We could retire in Jamaica on $150,000. We could live like kings for that much. My boat and house will sell for about $60,000. We only need $90,000 more." Luisa said, "If I work about a month, we should have plenty of money." Jim said, "I would still need to drive the boat and manage Anita and Juanita." Luisa said, "That's fine with me. Maybe when they have enough money, they will go to Jamaica with us." Jim said, "We'll have to ask them. Tomorrow we can talk to them at breakfast. We are meeting at 9:00 o'clock A.M. at the tavern. We can explain to them that you want to be mine in a month. If they agree that you don't need to work with the men, you could take care of the laundry for all of us. It would give you something to do till we all stop working." Luisa said, "I'd be glad to do the laundry. We can spend your free time fishing and getting to know each other better." Jim said, "That sounds good."

They finished their breakfast and played cards while drinking Jack Daniels and coke. When they were a little drunk they took another shower together and then went to bed. Jim couldn't get enough of Luisa's firm voluptuous breasts. He caressed them periodically throughout the night.

Next morning, they all met at the tavern for breakfast as planned. When they were all together Jeff said, "I didn't get any rainbow trout yesterday. We'll need to do that today for sure." Bill said, "I agree. The trout are high on the agenda for today." Juanita said, "I'll try not to suck you into spending the whole day with me, Bill." Bill blushed a little and said, "Juanita, I'm not saying that you sucked me in. I want to spend time with you. Sucking has nothing to do with it. You can fish with us, in fact." Steve said, "What did I hear said about sucking? Is sucking going on?" Anita said, "Yes, Steve. Sucking is going on, but it isn't on you. Please don't get your hopes up." Luisa said, "Don't get anything up. Not yet." she giggled. She whispered in Steve's ear, "I'll take care of you on Monday. You will be first in line." Steve whispered back, "I'll hold you to that!"

Jim said, "As Luisa's manager I need to talk to this group in private." Steve said, "You can all sit over by the window. No one will hear you there if you speak softly." They all moved over to the window. Jim said, "Luisa wants to only work with the men for one month. Then she wants to be my woman only. She will do the laundry. I will continue to manage Anita and Juanita. Luisa will call Loreto and arrange for another girl to come and do the full treatment for the men." Anita said, "This is wonderful news. Quite frankly I was starting to think that the men might not want showers and massages if they could have the full treatment instead. We can wait till we settle in Fairbanks this November to get the replacement. I wouldn't mind starting the business up so that we receive our 50% cut, and then retire in January. Jim, you could manage a couple new girls for us. The rest of us could see the mountains together. In one year the girls could be on their own and keep all the money. You could find them another manager then if you want out."

Jim said, "Luisa and I want to move to Jamaica as soon as possible. We would like all of you to come with us. Living is cheap there, much like in Mexico." Jeff said, "We could find the new girls a new manager in January. He would have to be loyal to us. Do you know anyone we could trust, Jim." Jim said, "My brother, Bret, wouldn't double cross us. He would give us our percentage for the year. I'll call him today and see if he's interested." Jeff said, "Then we could all go to Jamaica." Juanita said, "I'm not so sure about Bill. Will he marry me?" Bill said, "Last night you really did suck me in. You won me over completely. I will marry you. I will stay here and never return to Indiana. If I never see my wife again, I won't feel sorry for her. I can do the whole divorce with a fax machine and Jeff's lawyer." Jeff said, "That's the spirit, Bill. Now you are starting to get your priorities straight." Bill said, "Something sure got straight last night." Juanita giggled and hugged Bill. She whispered in his ear, "It will be even better tonight. You will see." Bill smiled and hugged her.

Now that everything was taken care of . . . . Jeff called Steve over and they all ordered breakfast. Everyone had the bacon. It was delicious the day before. They each ordered eggs the way they liked them. Steve recommended his special that morning of cinnamon and raisin toast with butter to go along with the breakfasts. They each ordered several slices of the toast that was a rarity for that area. They all had coffee and orange juice. Juanita looked at Jim and then at Luisa. Jim said, "What is it, Juanita?" Juanita said, "Was Luisa that good, or were you that good, Jim? Why the sudden falling in love?" Luisa said, "He is excellent in bed and in the shower. I want a man like him who will appreciate me and treat me nice. He's very polite." Jim said, "I like the way Luisa really cares about what makes me happy. She isn't just out for her own pleasure. She wants to make me happy. That's important." Juanita said, "I was just curious. Those sound like very good reasons for falling in love. I'm jealous. It took me longer than that to win Bill." Luisa said, "Don't blame Bill. Maybe he had a good life in Indiana that he hated to give up. I didn't have a good life to leave behind." Juanita said, "That's right. He had to give up more."

Their breakfast came and they all ate with enthusiasm. Steve said, "It does my heart good to see people eating my food with so much gusto." Luisa said, "You just spoke some Spanish, Steve. When we like something, we say 'Me gusto mucho.' It means literally, 'I like much.' I will teach you more later." Steve said, "I've never heard Spanish around here. We need more nice Spanish girls up here like you." Luisa said, "I will be bringing some more soon. I only plan to work for one month. Then Anita and Juanita will do there type of work without me. In November some more girls will come from Mexico and work with the men in Fairbanks. In January we will all retire. The new girls will work along the river in the summer with Jim's brother most likely." Steve said, "That sounds good to me. We need something like that around here."

Jeff said, "We're all moving to Jamaica to fish for marlin and other smaller fish. Speaking of fishing, as soon as everyone is done eating, we need to go to the trading post and get some night crawlers. Those trout won't wait forever. Don't they bite best in the early morning and late evening? Jim said, "If we hurry, we can catch a few late risers. You're right though. They bite the best from 7:00 to 9:30 A.M. They bite again in the evening, but not as good as in the morning." Bill said, "Well, we can get up early tomorrow morning and catch plenty of them. We can still give it a try today, though."

They all finished their breakfasts and walked over to the trading post to buy some worms. A white haired man in his late 60s greeted them. He said, "I'm Otto Laurence, the owner. What can I do for you today?" Jeff said, "We want to fish for rainbow trout. Do you have any night crawlers?" Otto said, "I have plenty of them. How many do you want?" Jeff said, "I'd like two dozen of them." Otto used his cane to hobble to the back of the store. He had a white beard and moustache. He was a little heavy and was about six feet tall. The worms were in a refrigerator which was in the back room. Otto counted out two dozen worms and put the rest of them back into the refrigerator. Slowly he walked back to the front cash register. "Is that all for you?" he said. Jeff said, "That should do it for today." Jeff paid for the worms and they all left the trading post and went back to the boat.

Jim rigged up poles for everyone and they all fished for rainbow trout. Jim said, "They are down on the bottom of the river. We can fish right from the boat and pier." They all spread out along the pier and on the boat and started fishing with the night crawlers. In about 20 minutes Luisa had a fish on her line. She had never done much fishing before. Jim coached her on how to reel it in. She followed his instructions and reeled in the fish steadily without jerking the hook out of the fish's mouth. It turned out to be a nice three pound rainbow trout. Next, Jeff got a fish on. He played the fish for a long time. He didn't want to hurry the fish. His fish turned out to be a four pound rainbow. It made him very happy. That was the last fish that was caught in the morning. Jim took everyone for a boat ride. They rode upstream to the town of Pitkas Pt. and looked around that town for a little while. They went to the tavern and Jim set things up with the owner for the girls to work there on Wednesday and Thursday. The owner's name was John Wilson. He said, "I'm looking forward to having all of you here. Drinks are on the house for all of you." It was noon, and they all ordered Cheeseburgers with Jack Daniels and coke. Luisa asked John, "Do you have a bedroom and shower that we can use to work in." John said, "I have a nice cabin by the river that you can use." Luisa said, "That'll be nice. We usually start work at 2:00 o'clock in the afternoon." John said, "Fine then. I'll spread the word."

They ate their food and had several rounds of free drinks. Then they climbed back into the boat and rode a little further upstream. Jim said, "The next town is Pilot Station. It's about fifteen miles upstream. I don't think we want to go that far today. We'll be going there on Friday. I'll call ahead and make arrangements." Luisa said, "This is a nice boat. I like the way the engines sound. It seems powerful. Can we go faster?" Jim said, "I'll take it to full speed for a little while. It uses lots of gas when we do that." He gave the boat full throttle. Jim said, "See the speedometer? We're going 30 m.p.h. That is all she'll do. It's a heavy boat." Luisa asked, "Can I drive it?" Jim said, "I'll let you steer it for a little while. First I'll slow down a little." He brought the speed down to seven m.p.h. and then let Luisa steer. She said, "I like this boat. We should take it to Jamaica with us." Jim said, "That's a long way to go by boat. It would be about 5,000 miles. We might want to let a captain down there take us out fishing. It would be cheaper in the long run. Or we could buy a boat when we get down there." Luisa said, "That sounds good. We could buy a boat that's even bigger." Jim said, "If we all go in together and buy a boat, we could buy a 75 foot yacht or a 40 foot cruiser." Jeff said, "We could live on the yacht and fish off the cruiser." Jim said, "Now you're talking. That's an excellent idea."

Jeff said, "I think that before we move to Jamaica, we should all hike in the Kaiyuh Mountains in January. I'd like for the girls to find out what winter actually is." Jim said, "The temperature gets down to 60 below zero that time of winter. I don't think it's a good time to go. Late March would be a better time. In January we could all freeze to death." Jeff said, "We could return from Jamaica in late March. You know what's best, Jim." Anita said,

"I'd like to see the snow in the mountains up close. I've only seen pictures of it." Juanita said, "I think it's a great idea. We could all take lots of pictures." Luisa said, "It sounds good to me." Bill said, "I'll go, but it isn't the most thrilling thing I can think of. I prefer the warmth of Jamaica." Jeff said, "We could make the flight reservations for the last Monday in March." Jim said, "I'll take care of that. It will still be plenty cold then for everybody. We will need to watch out for wolves. They are everywhere in the mountains and all around Alaska. We can take our rifles." Bill said, "Now the trip is starting to sound more exciting. I think I'll do some more target shooting this week."

Jim accelerated the boat to 10 m.p.h. The golden sunshine reflected brightly off the rippled waters of the river. There were only a few white clouds in the late afternoon sky. They were only a few miles from St. Mary's when Jim slowed the boat. He said, "We could stop here to fish for rainbow trout. It would give us some different scenery to look at." Everyone agreed, and Jim anchored the boat. Jeff and Bill got out the poles and night crawlers. They all started fishing off the bottom. After about an hour the fish began to bite. This time everyone caught several fish. Jim put all the fish in his large ice chest that was on the deck. He said, "We can cook them this evening in butter and eat them with buttered bread." Luisa said, "You sure like butter, Jim." Jim said, "It's the way my mother cooked. I don't know of any other way to eat fish." Luisa said, "It's fine with me. I won't complain." They all kept peeking in at the beautiful fish. They had dark green and brown backs with blushes of pink on their sides. The bellies were white. Most of each fish's side was light green in color. There were black spots all over the fish. Its tail was spotted as well and had a slight fork to it. The eyes were green with large black pupils. Luisa said, "These fish are almost too beautiful to eat." Jim said, "Many people say that. They are nice to look at, that's for sure."

As the sun started to turn red and settle down over the horizon, Jim cleaned the fish. Everyone watched with interest, to see how he did it. His hands moved quickly and skillfully as he cut off the heads and gutted the fish. Then he removed the fins and scrapped the scales off with a spoon. He said, "For most fish, I take off the skin; but the skin of rainbows is attractive, and it tastes good too. He cleaned all the fish and then took them to the galley. He said, "The lights can't be left on too long when we aren't plugged in at the dock, but we can use the batteries for long enough to eat out here on the water." He turned on the stove and started to cook the fish. Everyone sat at the table in the galley and played cards while they waited for the fish to cook. They played strip poker. Every time someone lost a hand, they had to take off an item of clothing. In less then ten minutes the girls were all topless. Jeff and Bill were winning. They still had all their clothes. The girls were lucky that the fish got done cooking before they lost everything. They weren't too shy anyway. The men couldn't help but notice how firm and shapely the girl's breasts were. They all had nice small brown nipples that begged to be kissed. None of their breasts showed the slightest sign of sagging. The wonder of youth was still upon them. Their tummies were lean and smooth, with no rolls of fat. It was a truly inspirational sight to behold.

Jim said, "The fish are ready. Let's eat." He placed the fish on a platter and placed it on the table. Then he quickly set the table. When he finished setting the table, he set out a jug of milk and a bottle of whiskey. He said, "There is water too for anyone who wants it. He set the bread and butter on the table, and they all started eating. Jim said, "Watch out for the rib bones. These fish aren't filleted." Juanita said, "These are delicious!" She buttered some bread and folded it over her fish that she had deboned. Eagerly she ate the tasty morsels. Anita said, "This is the best food I have ever had. I like it better than lobster." Bill said, "You can't beat this trout for flavor." Luisa said, "I think we'll need to fish for rainbow trout every week. I will be wanting more of this." They all ate until they were full. After the meal they played some more cards and drank Jack Daniels and coke on ice. When the girls got drunk enough they got under the table and gave the presidential treatment to their men. The men went on playing cards with big smiles on their faces. They tried to keep on playing with straight faces, even when the girls succeeded in getting them off. Jeff said, "This is the most fun I've had playing cards for a long time." Bill said, "I like this too. It's just a little hard to concentrate on the game." Jim said, "I noticed that too."

About an hour later, the girls all came out from under the table. They were grinning and giggling. They each had a drink of whiskey and started playing cards again. Juanita said, "I hope that will make you sleep well tonight." Bill said, "I'm sure that I'll sleep like a baby." Jim said, "I'd better take the boat back to the pier. I don't want to run the batteries too far down." He started the boat and steered it back to St. Mary's. On the way back, the passengers all leaned on the gunnels and watched the quarter moon rising in the east. "These are different star constellations than we have in Indiana," said Bill. Jeff replied, "Yes, I don't recognize a thing up here." Luisa said, "The stars are nice and bright tonight. The clouds are gone now." She stood next to Jim as he steered the boat by moonlight. He moved slowly and watched for the lights on the pier. Finally he saw the lights, with their reflections glimmering across the gently rippling water. He pulled in smoothly and let Jeff and Bill hold the boat while he tied it fast to the pier.

They all played cards till 3:00 o'clock in the morning. The girls stayed topless since they knew that the men enjoyed looking at them that way. Finally they managed to finish off most of the bottle of Jack Daniels. Jeff said, "Well, I'm tired. I think Anita and I will go to the cabin and get some sleep." Bill said, "I'm tired too. Juanita, are you ready to go to the cabin?" She said, "Yes, I'm ready to go any time." Anita and Juanita put on their tops and the two couples went to their cabins.

Time passed quickly for the next 30 days. Luisa earned her money that she needed for Jim and her to retire. She did the laundry and fished with Jim for the next seven months, while Anita and Juanita earned their retirement money. The Fairbanks massage parlor was run by Jim's brother. Luisa brought up some of her friends to take over for Juanita and Anita when they were finished in January. Jim sold his boat and house and Jeff sold his car. The whole group flew to Loreto to visit Carlos and Maria.

CHAPTER FIVE

The Retirement Experience

Carlos and Maria were waiting for them at the airport in Loreto. They were driving the motel's Chevy van. When they saw Juanita, Anita, Jeff and Bill, they ran up and hugged them all. Maria said, "I haven't seen you for so long! You left at the end of April last year." Juanita said, "We're glad to be back. Is there room in the motel for us?" Maria said, "There's plenty of room. I have the second motel now. It's working out fine for me." Anita said, "We're all rich now. We're going to retire in Jamaica." Maria said, "Jamaica! Why not stay with me." Anita said, "We want to try something different." Jeff made some introductions, "This is Jim Andrews, and you know Luisa. They are a couple now." Maria said, "It's good to meet you, Jim." Carlos said, "Good to meet you, Jim." Carlos said, "If you'll all get in our van, we can go to the motel and talk over supper." They all got in the van and went to the motel. While they sat at supper they discussed Jamaica. Luisa said, "We have enough money between us to buy a nice house, a 75 foot yacht and a 40 foot cabin cruiser. We want to enjoy living on the big yacht and fishing on the cruiser." Juanita said, "We have enough money now to retire on. We won't need to work. We can just travel and fish. The men like to hunt too." Jeff said, "In late March we are going to the Kaiyuh Mountains in Alaska to hike and camp. The girls want to try winter camping. I wanted to go in January, but Jim said it's too cold then."

Jim said, "In a couple days we are going to Jamaica to find a house. We'll buy the boats after we move into the house. We want to find something close to a marina that is right on the beach." Luisa said, "I'm sure we can find something, since we have the money to buy even a rather expensive house. It will need to be big, for all of us to live there comfortably." Jim said, "Tomorrow morning I'll make the flight reservations for us. We'd like to be in Jamaica Monday, January 5th. That way we can shop for houses early in the week and possibly move in the same week. This is Saturday, so we can spend Sunday here and leave the next day." Carlos said, "I wish you could all stay longer, but I know you are anxious to find that new house. We can go for a boat ride tomorrow and eat on the boat." Jeff said, "That sounds like a great idea. I missed the boat and fishing here on the Sea of Cortez. I'm sorry that we're in such a hurry. We'll come to visit once we have our house and boats purchased." Anita said, "Yes, We'll visit often. Don't worry about that."

Maria said, "Let's go down by the shoreline and sit in some lawn chairs. I'll have someone set them up and bring us drinks." Juanita said, "That sounds like a good idea." They all walked slowly down to the shore and talked about how things had gone during the last year. The sun was setting and spreading an orange glow over the palm trees and beach. The white motel especially reflected the color of the sun as it slowly dropped over the horizon. They could feel the last bit of warmth from the sun as it shown on their backs. They looked to the east, out across the sea. The motel workers brought out the chairs and everyone ordered drinks. They sat and listened to the waves. The wind was mild, but strong enough to cause the waves to speak with a splashing sound on the beach that was pleasant to the ear. Carlos said, "I think tomorrow will be a nice day for boating. It's supposed to stay calm, according to the weather report." Bill said, "Maybe we could catch a few red snappers." Carlos said, "If you want to, we certainly can." Maria had the motel workers build a nice bonfire down by the beach. They all had exotic tropical fruit drinks and talked around the fire till it was late. The sparks from the fire were beautiful as they leaped into the air and soared skyward. The fire crackled and popped loudly. Gradually they all fell asleep by the fire.

In the morning, the sun started to climb from the edge of the Sea of Cortez. It woke all the fireside sleepers. They went into the motel and showered. They were so tired that they drank coffee in the shower. Afterwards they went to breakfast and had bacon with pancakes and maple syrup. As they sipped more coffee around the breakfast table, they talked about Jamaica. Juanita said, "I hope we find a big house with lots of bathrooms." Luisa said, "I would like a sauna and hot tub. We could have them added if they're not in the house we buy." Jeff said, "I like that idea, Luisa. A steam sauna would be wonderful." Anita said, "We could add a swimming pool if there isn't one already." Bill said, "I would like a nice library or living room with large windows looking out over the ocean. I could read there." Carlos said, "Maria and I will come to visit you. We want to see this wonderful house." Maria said, "Yes, I'm sure you will find something beautiful. If not, you could always have a house custom built for you. Have you decided what part of Jamaica to live in?" Bill said, "We looked at some maps on the internet. We'll fly to Montego Bay and look around that area for a house. The Montego Bay Yacht Club is near the airport. It would be a convenient area to live in. We could dock our boats at the Yacht Club and stay in a house nearby." Anita said, "The club is close to several nice beaches. There is the Walter Fletcher Beach; which is on the north side of Montego Bay. The Doctor's Cave Beach is less than a mile further north, and Cornwall Beach is a little further north from Doctor's Cave."

Luisa said, "Montego Bay is on the north side of Jamaica. It is about 35 miles from the furthest western point of the island. The island is only about 66 miles long from east to west; and 22 miles thick in the middle running north and south. It lies just south of Cuba." Maria said, "It sounds like you have all done your research. I'm sure you'll find a nice house. Tell me more about Jamaica." Luisa said, "There is a mountain at the eastern end of the island. It's over 7,000 feet high and is called Blue Mountain. We want to climb it and possibly build a cottage near the top. We might decide to use Jeff's big tent instead of building a cottage. I'm sure that the view from up there will be a wonderful thing to see. The ocean wouldn't be far away. We will be able to see it well, from the mountain top." Carlos said, "You had better buy some burros. It will be a lot of climbing to get to the top of such a mountain." Juanita said, "Burros would be a good idea. We'll need to take lots of supplies up the mountain. Who wants to carry all that stuff?"

Anita said, "I read on the internet that most of the farms in Jamaica are under 10 acres. They measure the land in hectares. One hectare is 2 ½ acres. 55% of the meat grown in Jamaica is chickens. 20% of the meat is beef. Most of the beef is raised on big 40 hectare farms where they grow nothing but beef. Jamaicans only produce 14% of the milk they consume." Maria said, "You learned a lot about Jamaica. Did you print out any maps?" Anita said, "Detailed maps cost quite a bit of money. I was only able to get basic maps with the major towns shown. I am still trying. Maybe you can help me tonight on your computer." Maria said, "We can do some searching. Who knows what we may find?" Juanita said, "I wonder if mosquitoes are a problem on the beaches and in the mountains." Bill said, "We'll have to find out the hard way. If there are lots of mosquitoes, we'll have to make sure there are window screens in the home we buy." Juanita said, "If there are lots of mosquitoes, I may vote for us to live on an island where there are no mosquitoes, or we could come back to Loreto. We have few mosquitoes here."

Carlos said, "If everyone is done eating, we could take the boat out for a cruise and do some fishing." They all got up and followed Carlos to the boat. It was already loaded with food, drinks, ice and bait. Jeff and Bill untied the boat and got in. Carlos drove them out to his favorite fishing spot. He anchored the boat, and they all began to fish for red snapper. In no time at all, they were pulling in some nice fish. Each snapper had a nice red color to it. They bent the pole nicely as they were reeled in. Jeff said, "I'd guess that our biggest snappers weigh about 10 pounds each." Carlos got out the scales and weighed them. Sure enough, the biggest ones were between nine and eleven pounds." Everyone took part in the fishing. They all caught their limits in about another three hours. They put the fish on ice, and Carlos took them for a long cruise along the shoreline. They saw a few nice homes along the shore, but most of the beach was undeveloped. Juanita said, "If there are lots of mosquitoes in Jamaica, we can build something nice along this coastline." Bill said, "We will have to wait and see. Tomorrow we will be in Jamaica. We can see for ourselves how things are along the beach and on the mountain."

They cruised along the coastline until the sun started to get low in the sky. Carlos turned the boat back for home. He drove a little faster, so that they wouldn't get caught out in the darkness. Maria whispered in Carlos's ear, "Why don't we sleep out on the water tonight. It would bring back some nice memories. I brought three big blankets along." Carlos said, "I'll run the boat slower. We can stay in sight of the lights of Loreto." As the boat slowed, Anita asked, "Why are you slowing down, Carlos?" He said, "Maria thinks that you would all like to stay on the boat tonight." Anita said, "That's a wonderful idea. Things could get very presidential." She and Juanita giggled and hugged their men. Maria gave Carlos a wink and squeezed his hand. Maria said, "Who would like a drink? Juanita, help me make some Jack Daniels and coke for everyone." Juanita said, "I'll help you." In a matter of minutes everyone was sipping on a drink and watching the sun as it dropped over Loreto. The desert sands turned a golden orange and reddish hew. There were a few scattered clouds on the horizon that scattered the rays of the sun in a spectacular way.

The golden light reflected off the white panga as it drifted in the ever so gentle breeze. As the last rays of light were leaving the western horizon, and the stars were starting to appear in the sky, Maria passed out the blankets. For hours the blankets gave the privacy the couples wanted as they brought back fond memories of their first times together on that boat. The waves lapped gently against the boat. The full moon shined bright across the water as it started its nightly climb up from the eastern horizon. Jeff thought to himself, "Anita is nice to have around, but I could really use her money. Possibly something will happen to her in the Alaskan mountains this coming March. Either way I win. I'm can't believe that I'm actually a little bit attached to her. That's not like me. I always saw my first wife as a means to an end. I got sex and housekeeping. When the sex was gone, I got rid of her. The same sort of thing would happen if I lived with Anita very long. Women don't take long to go sour after marriage. It will be a relief when I can fish around the world alone with all that money."

After a late evening of love making, the passengers fell asleep. Carlos kept one eye open to make sure that the boat didn't drift too far from Loreto. When the sun started to rise, he started the engine and steered the boat back to the pier. They all ate breakfast together and then packed for the flight to Jamaica. As they loaded their suitcases into the van, they discussed the future. Juanita said, "I sure hope the insects aren't a problem. If they are, we may decide to move back to Loreto." Maria said, "You can always spray for insects." Juanita said, "I'll leave that up to the men. I don't know anything about that." Bill said, "We can hire people to spray for us. Just so they don't over do it and make us sick. I'm not against the idea of moving back to Loreto if the insects are too bad in Jamaica." Jeff said, "I don't like insects either. We could shop around for an island property somewhere where there are no bad insects like mosquitoes." Bill said, "I heard that Bimini is a good island to live on. They have few insects and good fishing. Things are more expensive there though. It's an island that gets plenty of tourist dollars, so they are used to charging more for things." Anita said, "That doesn't sound too good. We would be better off living in Loreto." Bill said, "We'll just have to take this all one step at a time. We can rent property till we are sure where we want to live."

They continued the discussion all the way to the airport. They got there just in time to board their plane. Everyone said their goodbyes and then the travelers boarded the jet. Their tickets were first class, so they were guided to the first class compartment. It was roomy and the seats were far apart. They were all given free drinks and snacks. Since their flight wasn't a long one, they didn't eat a meal on the plane. In a couple hours they were landing at the Montego Bay airport. They took a limo to the Montego Bay Yacht Club. It was only a few miles from the airport. At the club they went to the front desk and asked about renting three rooms with views of the water. They were quickly accommodated. The porters carried the luggage and moved them into their new quarters. Jim called a car rental place and had a van delivered. They all climbed inside and went to the Banco National to get some currency exchanged and to move some money form their bank in Alaska to that bank. In less than an hour, they were on their way to see Jamaica. They went to a grocery and bought a cooler and filled it with enough food for the day. They also bought some Jack Daniels and coke, which they put on ice. They bought paper cups and plates. Jeff said, "We should be around here this evening to see how the mosquitoes are in the area where we might want to live." Jim said, "We have all afternoon to drive around till then. Why don't we go to Negril? It's the furthest point to the west on Jamaica, and it's only about 35 miles from here." Anita said, "It's as good a place to start sight seeing as any. Let's go."

They all got in the white Chevy van and headed for the western town of Negril. They drove slowly and took in all the scenery. There were lots of trees and green bushes with brightly colored flowers on them. The flowers were pink and purple. Some were red. There were hundreds of flowers on each bush. They stopped every couple miles so Bill could take pictures. The road was rough for most of the way to Negril. The country side was full of small farms where lots of chickens could be seen everywhere. There were some pigs too. Only a few sheep and goats could be seen. People were riding bicycles along the road.

When they arrived in Negril, they found that it was geared towards tourists. The town had a nice white sands beach which people told them was seven miles long. They stopped at the marina and asked about prices for boats and mooring fees. Jim said, "Prices are a little lower here since it is not as popular as Montego Bay. Maybe we should stay here till evening and see what the sunset looks like from the beach. The man at the desk says it's worth seeing. He says they spray regularly for mosquitoes here. The town council pays for it." Juanita said, "I'd like to see the sunset. We could have a picnic on the beach." They rented a room at the marina and put on swim suits they had brought with them. In no time they were all on the beach sunning themselves, drinking mixed drinks and playing cards. They didn't even notice the sun was getting closer and closer to the water. Evening was approaching. They started to sense the immense beauty of the sunset that was forming. The purples and oranges reflected off the scattered clouds which were lingering on the horizon. Brilliant rays of white and gold could be seen, as the clouds deflected the sun's light. All the group watched intently as every change in the lighting took place. Finally, as the darkness moved, in Anita said, "I could enjoy living here. That is the kind of sunset a person would never grow tired of." Jeff said, "And I haven't heard any mosquitoes yet, or felt them." Jim stated, "Let's go to the local Yacht Club and see how the people are there." Jeff replied, "Yes, we can compare them to the people at Montego Bay and let that help us decide where to live." Bill added, "It sounds good to me."

They all got dressed in their street clothes and walked the short distance to the Yacht Club. They were greeted by a friendly hostess who wanted to know if they were members. Jim said, "We will be joining this week some time. We want to consider buying a house here and most likely a yacht and a power boat. Can you put us in contact with someone who is knowledgeable about such things?" The hostess said, "The club's owner, Mr. Martinez, is not busy right now. I'll ask him to meet you at your table to talk with you about those things." She had a waitress seat the group and then went for Mr. Martinez. They were seated at a window overlooking the ocean. The nearly full moon was lighting up the water. Jim ordered drinks for everyone and soon Mr. Martinez arrived and introduced himself. "I am Juan Martinez, the owner of the club. I hope I can be of service to you." They all introduced themselves. Mr. Martinez said, "There is little in the way of homes for sale here in Negril. We encourage people who are not citizens to rent a condominium. That reduces complicated paperwork. We want to keep the beach open to all visitors, so we don't sell waterfront properties to individuals." Jim said, "That is understandable. Are there plenty of condos available?" Mr. Martinez said, "We always have a few available. The cost is reasonable." Jim asked, "Are there many yachts and powerboats for sale here?" Mr. Martinez said, "The selection is limited. You'll find a much wider selection at Montego Bay. If you decide to stay in Negril, you could bring your boat here from Montego Bay." Jim said, "That sounds like a good idea. Thank you."

Mr. Martinez answered many more of their questions and then said, "I think you will find the club members here quite friendly. There is always someone who will want to take you fishing with them, and they will be eager to be guests on your boat as well. It was nice to meet all of you. I hope you will accept a complimentary dinner from the club. I am looking forward to seeing all of you again soon. Now I must excuse myself. I need to talk to some of our members." He smiled and shook the men's hands. He elegantly kissed the hand of each of the women. Then he left the table and disappeared from sight. Jeff said, "He was a nice man. It was generous of him to give us a free meal." The waitress appeared and took their orders. She said, "The special tonight is Bahamian lobster. You can have all that you can eat with real melted butter to dip it in." They all chose the special.

While they waited for their food they looked around at the club members. Everyone was dressed well, but not too formally. Many of the men wore expensive looking shirts that weren't tucked into the pants. The shirts were heavily embroidered and were cut straight across the bottom. Juanita said, "You don't see many shirts like those in Loreto." Jeff said, "I would like to have a few of them. They seem to be the things to wear here." Bill said, "I like those shirts." Juanita said, "We can buy some tomorrow. We can go shopping in Montego Bay."

Their food arrived. They all had salads and baked potatoes with the lobster. The waitress returned in a few minutes with a magnum bottle of expensive champagne from the Gallo vineyards. She said, "The gentleman and his guests at the table next to you want to welcome you to the Negril Yacht Club. His name is Fernando Gonzales. He owns the largest yacht at the Club's marina." They all looked over to where the waitress indicated. Fernando waved to them and smiled. The waitress poured out some champagne for Jim to test. He approved it. The waitress then poured them each a glass full. After they had finished their meal and the champagne, Fernando came over to their table and asked, "May I join you?" Jim said, "We would like to talk with you. Please sit down." Fernando was introduced to everyone. He said, "So, Luisa. You have my last name. Possibly we are related." Luisa said, "It is possible. We must compare relatives later." Fernando said, "Where are you staying tonight?" Jim said, "We have rooms rented at the Montego Bay Yacht Club." Fernando said, "You don't want do drive on those terrible roads tonight. Let me have one of my staff return your car to the club. I will give you a ride on my yacht to Montego Bay. I am excellent at night time navigation. You have nothing to worry about." Jim looked at the others. They all smiled. Jim said, "I think it is unanimous. We'll accept your invitation." They all followed Fernando to his table, where he introduced them to his wife, Anabel. She was a thin light skinned young woman who looked like she was about 25 years old. Her black hair was elegantly tied up in a bun. It looked like an expensive hair styling. She had on a yellow gown and wore a yellow flower in her hair. Fernando was about 50 years old and was six feet tall. He had black hair and a mustache. He was dressed in an expensive white suite with white leather shoes. He said, "If everyone is ready, we can go now. I will show you the way." He led them out of the club and over to the marina where his 100 ft. yacht was waiting.

Fernando said, "The yacht is called My Lady of the Sea. She has been with me now for five years. I only had to pay $2,000,000 for her. She is equipped with full night time navigation equipment. Radar, G.P.S., Sonar and all the radio equipment that anyone could ask for. She has a massive generator and can be lighted up like a small city." He took them on a short tour of the yacht and then started the engines. He said, "At night we will need to stay around six knots for our cruising speed. We should reach Montego Bay in about six hours." While Fernando personally steered the yacht, the others sat near him on chairs and asked him questions about living in Negril.

He knew much about the town. He said, "I have lived here for ten years. The sunsets are so wonderful here and the fishing is so good, I can't imagine wanting to live anywhere else. There is no crime here. Everyone who works in this town has enough money to live on. Nobody is desperate for money here. The farmers in the surrounding area are honorable and can be trusted. If you would decide to live in Montego Bay, you would need to worry about con artists. The wealth of that area attracts them. Negril is too small for such people. They would be found out." Jim said, "It sounds like you want us to move to Negril." Fernandez said, "I would invite you to my yacht often for fine dining and we could play cards. I always enjoy finding new fishing companions." Jeff said, "We are dedicating our lives to fishing and playing cards." Anabel said, "That is the kind of talk we like to hear." Fernandez said, "Yes, I will help you find a good yacht for a reasonable price." Jim said, "We only want to spend about $300,000 on a 75 foot yacht. We want a 40 foot power boat as well. We can spend around $80,000 on it." Fernando said, "I'm sure there are some older yachts and powerboats that are in excellent condition that will fit your price requirements."

Jim said, "We will have about $550,000 to invest after we buy the boats. We will have several hundred thousand more in a year from now. We don't want to risk loosing the money, but we would like a high rate of return. Do you have any ideas, Fernandez?" Fernandez thought for a minute and then said, "You need to diversify. I would put 30% in bonds for security. Place 40% in H____ywell. They will be doing well with all the wars I see likely to take place in the near future. Place the rest in my favorite mutual fund; New Dimensions Y. It netted me over 30% annual return during 1997 and 1998. Returns have been lower lately, but it is still the best thing going. I can almost guarantee you a combined return of 18% with this investment strategy. But as with all free advice, you have to personally accept all the risk." Jim said, "Thanks for the advice. Can I use your broker? We don't have one, now." Fernandez said, "Certainly. I'll see that there are no fees. With the volume of business I do with my broker, he can afford to be generous." Jim said, "I just want to know that our money will keep us from needing to work for a living. We may need to replace the boats every ten or fifteen years." Fernandez said, "It is wise to plan ahead like that. No one wants to retire and then find they needto go back to work. How did you all get your money in the first place?" Jim said, "I inherited it from my uncle. He liked me because I took him fishing a lot. His family got rich on gold in Alaska during the gold rush of forty-nine."

Fernandez said, "I made my fortune pedaling my wife's ass all over the Caribbean." He laughed, but stopped abruptly when his wife gave him a dirty look. He said, "No, seriously. I have had to set up hundreds of manufacturing deals between United States companies and China to make my fortune. I am partly responsible for most items in American stores being manufactured in China. I am currently setting up hundreds of publishing deals between the two counties. The cost of publishing books in America has made that a fertile ground for my brand of profit making. I should net several million from that area alone this year. My own war oriented stocks will net me ten to twenty million when the next war takes place. I am predicting North Korea. They are in the news all the time. It is preparation for the inevitable. I write the white house every week to encourage an attack on North Korea. The United States and Britain can't police the whole world, but at least they can rid the world of those totalitarians. How dare they threaten the United States with their supposed newly found atomic weapons? We need to nip them in the bud."

Jeff said, "What if China supports the North Koreans? We could be starting the last world war." Fernandez said, "The Chinese know which side their bread is buttered on. They won't interfere with our attack on North Korea." Jeff said, "It just worries me that we are starting too much around the world. Why don't we just concentrate on controlling terrorism?" Jim said, "None of us will live forever. I agree with Fernandez. We need to attack North Korea if they don't give up the atomic weapons." Bill said, "I think North Korea is too much like North Vietnam. We don't do too well in jungle warfare. We need to stick with desert wars. The world's oil supply is the only thing that is important. We can keep North Korea under control with star wars weapons. They are getting better all the time." Anabel said, "No more talk of war. Let's all have another round of Jack Daniels and coke. Juanita tells me, that's what all of you drink." Fernandez rang a bell, and a steward appeared. He took their order and reappeared moments later with the drinks. After the drinks, the talk moved to fishing. Jeff said, "What is the best kind of fishing here, in your opinion, Fernandez?" He said, "Jamaica has the best blue marlin in the world. They are bigger and more plentiful here than anywhere else. We have world class tournaments here. You must let me take you fishing for blue marlin this week." Jim said, "We are eager to go. You don't fish in this yacht, do you?" Fernandez said, "I have a 50 foot cruiser docked in Negril. We can go out tomorrow if you would all like to. I can pick you up in the morning. My wife and I will just stay on the yacht while you sleep in your rooms in Montego Bay. We will pick you all up in the morning." Jim said, "That will be fine. 8:00 o'clock would be a good time to come for us. We don't mind missing a little sleep for a day of fine fishing."

The next day everyone woke up early and got back on the Gonzales yacht. They enjoyed breakfast with Anabel, as Fernando steered the yacht back to Negril. Anabel took breakfast up to Fernando. He said, "We have servants to do that. Why do you carry food around like a servant?" Anabel said, "I like to serve you. You are my husband. This is how I show my respect." Fernando said, "You are always right. Why do I argue with you?" He leaned over and kissed her on the cheek. When they arrived at the marina, everyone left the yacht and got in Fernando's power boat. He steered them to his favorite fishing area. They took turns fishing for blue marlin. The fish were plentiful and everyone got to catch one. They reeled them in just like they did the blue marlin in the Sea of Cortez. Most of them were around 150 to 180 pounds. They were beautiful fish. Their dorsal fins spread out like sails. Their bodies glistened with black and shades of blue.

Fernando took them fishing every day for a week. During that time he also helped them buy their yacht and power boat. The yacht was 75 feet long and white like Fernando's. The power boat was 40 foot long and white, with a dark blue stripe for the full length of it. Jim and Luisa lived on the power boat, and the other two couples lived on the new yacht. They named the yacht, "We Earned it" and the power boat was named, "Ephemeral Blessing". Fernando asked, "Who named the power boat?" Anita said, "I did. Nothing is forever. We can't count on enjoying our wealth forever." Fernando said, "That is very true. We can't take it with us. Each day must be enjoyed. It could be the last day."

They all fished together and sailed until March. Then Jeff reminded them, "We were going to camp in the Kaiyuh Mountains, remember?" Luisa said, "That sounds good to me. It will be fun to experience the snow after all this tropical weather." They all agreed that it was time to go camping in Alaska. They booked their flights and left the next morning from Montego Bay Airport. Jeff had his cell phone and called ahead to Kaltag to arrange for the gear for the trip to be readied. He also arranged the flights from Anchoage to Kaltag. It would take two planes to haul all of them to the small town along the Yukon River. It was the closest town to the Kaiyuh Mountains. The next day was Tuesday, and they arrived at Kaltag with no problems. They rented snowmobiles to get them to the base of the mountains. From there they carried their small lightweight tent and backpacking equipment. They had to walk with snow shoes, since the snow was still several feet thick. It was sunny and in the 40s as they started up one of the mountains. It was a gradual climb and they were making good progress. Jeff said, "We have enough provisions for five days. We can hike up for two days. Stay a day, and then hike back down." Bill said, "That sounds like a good plan. I hope the weather stays nice like this. Jeff said, "I hope so too. This is nice weather for camping." Anita said, "I like using snow shoes. They force you to take your time." Juanita said, "I'm getting hungry. How long will we hike till we make camp?" Jim said, "We should be able to make it a third of the way up today. We won't want to try the last third. It is too steep for inexperienced climbers. We don't have the equipment for it anyway." Jeff said, "Even the middle third is a little treacherous. We'll need to watch our steps and not lose our balance."

Since there were lots of daylight hours in Alaska at that time of year, they had plenty of time to climb the first third of the way up the mountain. When they felt they had gone far enough, they stopped and made camp. The men pitched the tent, while the women made some coffee and hot food. After a much needed meal and some coffee, they spread out their sleeping bags. They all took their boots off and their outer clothing, but they left their long underwear on. It was too cold to sleep naked as they usually did. During the night they could hear the wind shaking their tent a little. Jim said, "It's just a little breeze. Nothing to worry about. Then they heard the howl of a wolf. Luisa said, "What was that?" Jim said, "There are wolves in these mountains. Don't worry, I brought a rifle." The wolf was quiet the rest of the night.

In the morning, they all woke early and saw the sunrise. It was great to see all the trees and the Yukon River stretched out below. They broke camp and headed on up the mountain. At noon the wind picked up a little and the sky started to darken with snow clouds. It was getting colder at the higher elevation. They all walked faster, so they would stay warm. At supper time they stopped to make camp. It was starting to snow heavily. They put up the tent and had their supper. They made pancakes with syrup. They had brought some kindling along for a fire. They chopped down a few of the local small trees and built a nice fire. They huddled around the fire and watched the snow falling heavier and heavier. Then they heard the calling of several wolves. The calls were closer than before. As darkness set in, the girls were afraid. Anita said, "What if they attack while we are sleeping?" Jim said, "We'll take turns staying awake with the rifle. One will hold the rifle and another will make sure he doesn't go to sleep." They took turns keeping watch all night. No one got much sleep. Juanita said, "I think we should go back in the morning. I don't like this. I'm too afraid of the wolves." Jim said, "As soon as it's light enough we can go." Jeff said, "I enjoy being up here. The snow worries me though. I guess we should go." Bill said, "I'm ready to go any time.

As the morning started to get light enough to see, they broke camp and headed back down the mountain. In the heavy snow they got a little off course. They couldn't see the tracks they had made on the way up. Anita didn't see the edge of a cliff coming up. She walked right off it and fell 100 feet onto a rock and split her head wide open. Bill tried to get to her and he too fell to his death. They were all in shock about the tragedy and decided to make camp right there. They couldn't try to retrieve the bodies or they too would die. It would need to be done later after the snow storm. Jeff thought to himself, "Now I am a rich man, but I didn't count on losing my best friend too." He felt some sincere remorse at the loss he had just experienced. Jim wouldn't give up trying to reach Anita and Bill. He couldn't believe that they were both dead. As he tried to climb down to them, he lost his grip. He and the rifle went tumbling off the cliff.

Jeff decided that it was time to use the cell phone and call for a helicopter and a rescue team. He opened the phone and discovered that it was dead. He was starting to experience fear. He hid it as best he could. Jeff said, "I think we should head down the mountain as fast as we can. This snow could get even worse." Juanita said, "I just want to get out of here." Luisa said, "I can't believe that all this is happening to us. What did we do wrong? Are we cursed?" Jeff said, "Let's get going. Don't get worked up worse than you are." Luisa said, "I'm not worked up. I really think we are cursed." Juanita said, "I think so too. Things this bad don't usually happen to campers. The wolves are closing in, and everyone is slipping off cliffs. How can we get through this?" Jeff said, "Just follow me. Stay right behind me. Don't go to the right or the left." They all started hiking down the mountain. They left most of the gear behind. Anita, Bill and Jim had been carrying the food. They couldn't retrieve it. All they had was the tent and some kindling for a fire. They walked as fast as they could in the snow shoes. Jeff could tell which way was down hill, but he couldn't see very far.

Suddenly something dark swished by them. It was a wolf. It let out a howl. Soon they were surrounded by wolves. Jeff tried to fight them, but they bit his wrists every time he swung at them. Finally he fell down and was attacked by five or six wolves at once. They ripped his coat into pieces and then tore open his belly. He was still alive as he watched each wolf run off with a long piece of his intestines. Slowly he died with his eyes wide open in horror.

The girls saw it happen and went into shock. They lay there in the snow unconscious. For some reason the wolves didn't touch the two girls after they fell unconscious. They contented themselves on continuing to feed on Jeff. The rest of the pack came and stripped him to the bones. The next morning Luisa and Juanita awoke and started walking down the mountain. They made it almost to the snowmobiles. The wolves came back and tore Luisa to pieces. While they were eating her, Juanita made it the rest of the way to the snowmobiles. She hopped on one and took off. When she got to town she told everyone what had happened. She said, "Someone in our group was cursed. I think it was Jeff. Bill told me that Jeff was hoping something would happen to Anita. He wanted her money. He was crazy. She was sharing her money with him anyway. Why was he against her. Now they are both dead and the rest of the group as well. God has punished us. He only left me so that I could tell the tale. I am the messenger. The greedy are punished. We angered God and he has struck."

No one contradicted her. She went back to Loreto and stayed at the Motel. She never worked with the tourists again. She only fished and thought of her loss. The money in the wills of Anita and Luisa stipulated that if Jeff and Bill did not live to inherit the money it would all go to protect whales.

The End

Printed in the United States
41578LVS00002B/243

9 781413 452808